ACES FULL

ALAN LEE

SPARKLE PRESS

Aces Full

by Alan Lee

First Edition
Printed in USA

Cover by Inspired Cover Designs

Formatting by Polgarus

Paperback ISBN: 978-1720304715

Sparkle Press

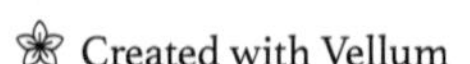

1

Grady Huff was gonna swing.

That's the way the Roanoke Times made it sound.

The man had no chance, guilty as sin, and soon he'd be strung up on a long rope on the tallest tree branch while the townsfolk watched.

Or sentenced to life in prison, but that was less romantic. Either way, Grady Huff's prospects looked grim.

I sat in my office, windows closed against a pale October chill, and read the Times on my laptop. My Merrell all-terrain hiking shoes (worn in case I needed to chase a dastardly villain up a rugged mountainside) were crossed on my desk. My black NorthFace rain jacket (worn in case the mountainside pursuit took place in a lashing downpour) was unzipped. My salmon slim-fitted Neiman Marcus (worn in case I needed to impress fashion-conscious damsels during the soaked mountainside chase) was neatly untucked. And I, lantern-jawed and intrepid investigator, pursuer of fiends, did not want to help Grady Huff escape his destiny.

He was a trust fund kid, now thirty-five, and he'd inherited millions from his father's investment in Pepsi in the fifties. Grady had bought a mansion on Smith Mountain Lake, spent his days inebriated on his dock and large sailboat, until one day killing his cleaning lady during a drunken bout of violence.

I brought up her picture—she was a cutie.

I brought up his—he was not.

I lazily reached into the bottom drawer of my desk and fetched the nearly-full bottle of Johnny Walker Blue. Scrappy gumshoes had no business owning such a luxury so I nursed it carefully. Somedays I only popped the cork and smelled it. Today, though, I thought, today was a drizzly day and a good one to indulge.

I popped the cork. Brought the bottle to my lips. Took half a sip, rolled it around, and replaced the bottle again.

Mackenzie August, uncontrollable lush.

I punched keys on my MacBook and the screen changed to my email. The most recently received was from a lawyer. Asking for my help. Asking me to help her prevent Grady Huff from swinging by his neck until dead.

But I didn't want to. The attorney didn't pretend Grady was innocent. She didn't want help proving his blamelessness, but rather to prevent the carriage of justice.

Help me, Mackenzie August. You're my only hope.

Without you, this heinous and guilty man might get what he deserves.

I sardonically shifted to stare out the window and think sardonic thoughts about the mist.

"The cleaning lady," I muttered. "Who kills their cleaning lady?"

Everyone knew that cleaning ladies were universally

nice women. If I could afford one, I'd be exceptionally kind to her. Unlike Grady Huff, the caveman.

I breathed in deeply through my nose, enjoyed the potpourri's masculine aroma, and thought deep thoughts while slowly exhaling like a popped tire.

After a while, the wooden stairs leading to my second floor office creaked and strained.

A man named Carlos came in. I knew Carlos, a tall and beefy associate of Marcus Morgan. Carlos was adept at hiding bodies, that's what I knew. His head was shaved, his facial hair short and wispy and thin. He had tattoos on his neck and his forearms. He looked the way mobster muscle should, except his face didn't hold the meanness. A gentle hitman.

His jeans were black. His tight gray t-shirt strained at the biceps and neck.

Carlos dropped to his knees at my desk. Pressed his face into the wood, and balled fists and made a sobbing sound.

"Carlos," I said. "You look destroyed. Is someone larger and scarier than you about to burst through my door?"

He shoved a hand into his pocket and set a thick envelope of cash between us, without looking up.

"August. You must be purchased. *Por favor.*"

"Hired, you mean."

"He took her. She was taken and I...I do not know."

"Who took whom?" I said.

"Mi niña. She is gone."

I sat up straighter. Claims of child abduction called for more erect posture.

"Your daughter was kidnapped?"

"Sí."

"When?"

"*No sé*. I do not know where. And when. And who."

"What do you know?"

He got to his feet. Wiped his eyes. Collapsed into one of my client chairs. "My daughter. Isabella. She live in Méjico. With her tía."

"Her aunt."

"Sí."

"And someone took her."

He nodded, trying to regain composure. And failing.

"Could it be retaliation for your work with Marcus? Professional rivalry?"

He shook his head. Took two deep shuddering breaths. "Okay. You listen. You understand a coyote."

"A coyote, yes," I said. With a sinking feeling. "Someone you pay to smuggle yourself or a loved one across a boundary, like the Mexican border."

"Sí. I save money. I pay a coyote. He bring Isabella from Méjico. Across the border. I speak with her on the phone."

"And now the coyote wants triple the price or he won't release Isabella," I guessed.

"Not three. Four."

"Quadruple! And you don't know if Isabella is still alive. Or if he'll let her go even if you pay."

His eyes squished and his mouth turned down again. "Sí."

"Well damn, Carlos."

He reached forward to press the envelope closer to me. "Here. For you. You find her. And maybe I can get you a diamond."

"A diamond? Why don't you ask Marcus to help? He's got connections in the underworld."

"I will. If you can not. You understand? It is... It is..."

"Embarrassing and unprofessional?"

"Sí."

"When your daughter is missing, getting help is never embarrassing and unprofessional, Carlos."

He said, "Please, Seńor August."

"How old is Isabella?"

"Fourteen."

"Damn," I said again. "Any number but fourteen."

"You will help."

"Of course. *Por supuesto*. I owe Marcus multiple favors anyway." I closed my laptop screen. Grady Huff would have to wait until tomorrow. "You have a number to call?"

"After I have money, I call the number."

I stood up and removed my jacket. It wasn't raining indoors, Mackenzie, you idiot. I paced a moment. "Okay. You're going to take a photo of yourself with this stack of cash. Text it to that number. And then call."

"The coyote say PayPal."

"We're not doing PayPal. What kind of criminal does PayPal? Freaking millennials. You tell him you don't have PayPal, but you'll drop the cash anywhere. Tonight."

"Tonight?"

"Sí," I said. "This'll work better, we strike quick."

"Bueno."

"Shock and awe. A child is at stake. Tonight."

"Bueno! Esta noche. We do this now?"

"Yes. This very minute."

He grabbed the envelope and withdrew the cash. Spread the bills out in a fan in front of his face and snapped a pic with his phone. Replaced the cash into the envelope, set it on my desk, and sent the text message. "We will find him?"

"Yes," I said.

"I will kill him."

"Up to you. Wait a minute, let the coyote see the cash. Then call the guy. Put it on speaker."

Carlos nodded and watched his phone and sweated.

He lasted thirty seconds and then made the phone call.

"Remember," I told him. "No PayPal. You will drop the cash anywhere. Tonight. Has to be tonight. Follow my lead."

Carlos nodded and sniffed, the gentle hitman.

The phone clicked. A voice came over the speaker.

"Tienes listo mi dinero, migo?"

Carlos replied, "Quiero hablar con Isabella."

"No. Usted envía el dinero, recibe a su hija."

I was translating as best I could.

Something like, *you got the money?*

Yes, let me talk to Isabella.

No, only after I get the cash.

I made an angry face and balled a fist. Shook it at Carlos. Get mad!

Carlos nodded and yelled into the phone, "Mataste a mi hija! Que te jodan!"

"Isabella está viva. Relájate. No soy un asesino. Envía el dinero."

You killed my daughter!

No, she's alive. Send the money.

I nodded. Good. We'll give you the cash.

"Te traeré efectivo. Esta noche. Sin PayPal," said Carlos.

"Solo PayPal."

I shook my head. No PayPal.

Carlos said, "Efectivo. Esta noche. Sin PayPal. Lo dejaré en cualquier lado."

I'll bring you cash anywhere tonight. No PayPal.

"Tienes que usar PayPal, Carlos."

I shook my head and jumped. Swung my arms furiously. No PayPal, you piece of shit!

"No tengo PayPal, mierda!" Carlos shouted. "Efectivo. Esta noche! O te cortaré la garganta!"

"El punto es en Virginia Beach, Carlos. Usted conduce aquí esta noche?"

Cash tonight, or I'll cut your throat!

The drop is in Virginia Beach, Carlos. You'll drive here?

I nodded. Thumbs up. I whispered, "Tonight."

"Esta bien. Traeré el dinero. Y liberas a Isabella."

"Traes dinero esta noche? Voy a liberar a Isabella por la mañana."

I was getting a little lost. Something like, *I'll bring you the money tonight for Isabella.*

Then I will release her tomorrow.

I nodded. Big nod.

"Sí," said Carlos with relief. "Está mi hija en la playa de Virginia Beach?"

"Sí. Le enviaré un mensaje de texto con instrucciones."

Is my daughter in Virginia Beach?

Yes. I will text you with directions.

And he hung up.

Carlos set the phone down with shaking fingers. He squeezed his eyes shut again.

I patted him on his heavy shoulder. "Real good, Carlos. You did great. We're getting her back. Tonight."

"But the money. It's too much. I am not rich."

"We're not giving him a nickel. We're going coyote hunting in Virginia Beach. We're going to find the bastard and take Isabella by force."

2

Carlos left to pack a few things. Like a weightier gun.

I made a phone call.

The world's most mellifluous voice came on and filled my ear with steam and honey. "Hello Mackenzie."

"Hello Ronnie."

"Don't you find it strange that I've never seen you naked? Please send a nude photo this instant."

I said, "If you're with a client, he might be getting jealous."

"Or she."

I sat at my desk and reclined. "True."

"Do you remember Ruben Collier?"

"I do. Nice man. He tends the plantations of marijuana that you own."

"Oh my. Phrase that some other way. I've never seen the fields. I don't even know where they're located."

"He tends the plantations of marijuana that you inherited," I said. "But have never seen. He lives in Franklin County and is putting his kids through college by growing your major export."

"Ruben Collier called me. He requires my assistance making a few decisions about next year's crop and this year's stored surplus."

"What'd you tell him?"

"I told him I didn't have a clue! That I am an expert in civil law and trendy fashion," she said. "I need advice from someone I trust. Let's talk about my options over dinner."

"I need to cancel our plans tonight."

Her breath caught. "You're standing me up on our first date?"

"It wasn't a date and it wouldn't be our first. And yes."

"It *was* a date and I *was* going to throw myself at you," she said. "I purchased new lingerie."

"I do not date engaged women," I said. With a smile. A handsome and reticent one.

"That's over, Mackenzie. I just haven't told him. And I haven't seen you in weeks. What is so urgent that you torment me?"

"A child has been kidnapped. Only I can save her, hero that I am. I'll be gone until tomorrow."

Her breath caught again. I cherished that sound. "Okay, that's a good reason. I release you. What will you do with Kix, your perfect son?"

"Beg my father or Manny."

"I will watch him."

"Absolutely not," I said. "I've been inside your apartment. All your plants are dead."

"Because who cares about fucking plants. I adore your son and will remember to water him."

"Ronnie—"

I heard clicking sounds through the phone. She said, "I'm already canceling my appointments for the rest of today, Mackenzie. And tomorrow."

"You're going to be the world's hottest babysitter."

"Correct."

"You cannot take him to your place. You have to stay at mine."

"Finally," she said, "You ask me to sleep over. And you'll be out all night. Will Manny be there?"

"If he is, you may not touch him."

"When do you need me?"

"As soon as possible," I said. "We've not a moment to lose."

"I wish you were always this insistent. I'll see you soon, Mackenzie. And I expect payment up front."

AT MY HOUSE I threw a handful of granola bars into a backpack. Plus some water bottles and a box of .45 ammo. Kix drank milk and watched me with concern from his playpen, eyebrows raised over sparkling blue eyes.

Looks like you have a wild night planned.

I said, "Daddy's got to go out tonight, but he'll be safe."

Please don't refer to yourself in the third person. It makes things weird.

"Ronnie volunteered to watch you. Be a good boy."

Stay as long as you like, old man. The hot blonde and I will be juuuust fine.

Manny came home at four, as he often did, the captain of industriousness. An absurdly handsome and fit man, built like a wide receiver. He paused on the way to the fridge to glance in my backpack. "Señor, who you be shooting? Five hundred times, looks like."

"You know Carlos? One of Marcus Morgan's guys?"

"*Simon*, I know Carlos."

"He's being extorted by a coyote with his daughter. We're retrieving her."

He cocked a hip and crossed his arms. Inspected me with strenuous disapproval. "You and I, Mack," he said. "We no longer amigos?"

I grinned. "You want to go?"

He glared.

I said, "You can go but we'll be gone all night."

"That is a hell of a thing to say to me, cabrón."

"The coyote is in Virginia Beach, we think. The plan is, bust his door down. Then duck and shoot back, long enough to get the girl. You in?"

He didn't move. Glared some more. Then pointed a finger at me (which I knew for a fact had been manicured). "Next time you pack for a shootout without telling me? I shoot you myself."

"I apologize for not inviting you to get killed tonight by Mexican coyotes. Will never happen again. You big baby."

"You and me, we are Mack and Manuel. We work together. Like the candy, M&M. Everyone calls us that," he said.

"No they don't."

"Not if you keep taking Carlos and not me, stupid Anglo."

"Get your stuff," I said.

"I drive. My stuff is in the car."

Carlos arrived in an old grey Toyota pickup and parked on the street. Manny and I met him outside. The low grey clouds were lightening.

Manny called, "Pon tus bolsas en la parte trasera, amigo mío, e iremos a matar al jodido coyote."

Something about, *Put your stuff in my car and we'll go kill the coyote.*

"Hey, talk American," I said.

Carlos didn't move. "Señor August, we are taking the marshal?"

"We are," I said. "He's good at this."

"That's more like it," said Manny.

"And if we don't, he'll throw a hissy."

"I'm driving. Get us there quick."

Carlos looked at the black Camaro and shook his head. "Two doors? I do not fit."

"Ay dios mio," said Manny. "Fine. We'll take Mack's pretty Accord. But I drive."

A dazzling red Mercedes purred down the street. Parked in front of my house. And a dazzling blonde unfolded from the passenger door.

"Hello boys," said Ronnie.

She still wore her work outfit. If she hadn't been the proprietor of the office, her boss would've objected to the length of her grey skirt. Or tried to seduce her out of it. It had stopped drizzling but she popped an umbrella and walked my way.

An enormous man named Fat Susie got out of the driver's seat and shot us three guys a nod. He went to the Mercedes's trunk and fetched Ronnie's overnight bag.

Manny nodded back. "Hola, Fat Susie."

I said, "Why is Fat Susie driving you around?"

Ronnie shrugged, a motion that always looked good on her. Especially in this spaghetti-strap blouse.

She said, "A grumpy man is mad at me for some nonsense. Or so Marcus Morgan says, and he let me borrow Reginald."

Manny said, "The hell is Reginald?"

She stopped when our toes touched. We were very close,

her breath on my neck, whispers of her blonde hair tickling my chin.

"Ronnie," I said.

"Yes Mackenzie."

"It's nice to see you."

She raised up further on her toes and kissed me. My chin and then my lower lip. "I know."

"Why don't you kiss the other guys?"

"You owe me for babysitting. That's why," she said. "And you're supposed to kiss me back."

"But they're watching."

"Prude."

I opened the door for her and she and I went inside. She stepped out of her heels, a motion I could watch all day, and set the umbrella by the door.

She said, "Holy shit I love this house. I'm struck by it every time."

"Who is mad at you?"

"I'm not sure. It has to do with Ruben and marijuana and possibly men in Washington. Who cares. Marcus is taking care of it. That man is in a precarious position."

"He wants out of his position," I said, "He should quit shoveling cocaine around."

Kix made a loud sound, demanding to be noticed from his playpen. When Ronnie did, he beamed and jumped.

I knew the feeling.

She scooped Kix. "Look at this perfect angel baby. I could eat him."

"Kix thinks you're dressed a little scandalous for crawling on the floor babysitting."

"I brought a change of clothes, Mackenzie. I've done this before. I had to pay for my own car and cell phone in high school, and I did so by tending children."

"Are you wearing your new lingerie?"

"I am. Care for a glimpse? A tease?"

My chest tightened. A feeling like thirst and hope blossomed somewhere inside the inner recesses of my sensorium.

I sighed. "I would like that more than all things. But... better not. I wouldn't be able to aim tonight."

I showed her the diapers and the baby food and the fruit and the books and the baby clothes. Not nearly as much fun as lingerie modeling.

When I finished, she said, "You have not mentioned my glowing skin. Go on, try to find a blemish. You cannot."

"You've always been without blemish."

She reddened a little. "I recently returned from a week's stay at a spa. Sonesta, on Hilton Head. Mackenzie, it was paradise. I am a new woman."

"I didn't know you were a spa girl."

"I'm not. I went on doctor's orders," she said. "She said I wasn't allowed to take you."

"Doctor?"

"I'm in therapy. Twice a week."

"If I wasn't so manly, I might do a happy dance," I said. "A psychiatrist?"

"Kinda."

Kix regarded her suspiciously.

Kinda a doctor?

Ronnie said, "She's a...you're going to laugh."

"Not I. I do not laugh. I'm a big fan of physicians."

"She's a holistic psychotherapist."

"Oh," I said. "A witch doctor."

"No."

"A practitioner of voodoo. She lights incense and turns

on Coldplay and gives you kale and prescriptions to luxury resorts, and you're cured."

"You be kind. Besides it's not even Coldplay."

I said, "I'm sure detoxifying through a diet of homemade hemp enemas and aura cleansing will help you recover from twenty years of abuse."

Her shoulders fell and she lost some of her light. "I'm trying, Mackenzie. This is new for me."

"You're right." I winced. Mackenzie August, major league butthead. "I went too far. I am an ass."

She nodded.

Kix scowled at me.

I said, "I apologize. This is new for me too. I have a vested interest in your recovery, but...I shouldn't. I'll be a Ronnie fan no matter what, even if you go to New York Mets fans for advice on sexual healing."

"No one is that stupid."

"Amen."

She said, "Also, I'm not interested in having you for a fan. A groupie, maybe..."

I said, "You're engaged to another man."

"Ugh! Mackenzie! Stop bringing him up. Marcus asked me to give him a few more days to prepare before I tell Darren. That I'm leaving him. For greener pastures."

"My pastures are green as heck."

She smiled, a wicked twist on her perfect mouth. "You keep turning me down and I'll graze elsewhere and send you nude selfies as punishment. Every. Single. Night."

My son made a gasping noise.

"Kix just lost his innocence," I said.

"I can't wait to take yours. Is it Carlos's kid who got kidnapped, by the way?"

"His daughter."

"Poor guy. I like Carlos. Make sure you find her."

Fat Susie came in with Ronnie's bag. He looked around my house and nodded approval.

I said, "Your name's Reginald?"

"Fat Susie my middle name."

I kissed Kix on the forehead. Then kissed Ronnie's forehead.

"Take Manny," she said. "You'll be safer."

"I am."

"It's like we're a family. You go off to kill people and I'll stay home, barefoot, with Kix," she said.

"Our pretend family is whack. My father will be home soon, perhaps with the sheriff."

"Ooo, kinky."

3

We went up Interstate 81 and caught 64 East. Why not take 460, you ask? Is it not the more direct route? Manny wanted long straight stretches to go ninety miles per hour, that's why.

"We get pulled over," he said. "I show my badge. Good to go."

"Do not get pulled over. My weapons are not legal," said Carlos.

"Relax, hombre. We good. I play the Marshal card, we can do anything."

I rode in the passenger seat and acted as disc jockey. We alternated between reggae, mariachi, Frank Sinatra, and the Killers. Carlos shifted uneasily in the back the entire trip, glaring and grinding his teeth.

"This will not work," he kept saying. "This is *loco*."

Thirty minutes outside of Norfolk, I called an associate named Peter. Peter the Private Detective. He worked in this area.

He answered, "It's late, August. I'm on a hot date."

"You lie."

"This important?" he asked.

The connection wasn't great. Some static.

"What are you doing on your hot date?"

"Watching a damn romantic comedy at the theater. Actually, talk as long as you need, I'm ready to shoot myself in there," said Peter the Private Detective.

"I'm inbound, looking for a girl being held by a coyote out of Mexico."

"Yuck," he said.

"Yuck indeed."

"Need help? This movie's awful. Not sure my date's hot enough to warrant the pain."

"I got help. Looking for a starting point. There's no way the girl's working yet," I said.

In the back, Carlos groaned.

Peter made a throat clearing noise in the phone. "I don't know where these pieces of shit keep their girls. But I can get you started. Cops got wise on Backpage, put the heat on Portsmouth, so the action shifted. To, ahh—what's the name —to Ocean View. You know it? Drive up and down highway 60."

"The strip motels?"

"The Best Westerns, Express Inn, HoJo, Ocean View Inn, you know the kind of place. Motel 6. Pimps sit in the vans or SUVs or whatever."

"Ocean View. Thanks. That'll get me started," I said.

"Swing by and kill me on the way. This is the new movie with one of the Jennifers, you know? I can't keep 'em straight. Christ almighty."

~

AT 8PM, we turned onto highway 60 and motored south.

This was a good place to run cheap prostitution. Quiet but active, not far from the Navy base, close proximity to several beaches, tourist attractions like golf courses and botanical gardens. Good fishing everywhere.

Perhaps 'good place to run cheap prostitution' was the wrong phrase. Best not to get too cold, Mackenzie. Maybe instead, these conditions were ideal for traffickers looking to exploit prostitutes and lonely men.

We pulled into an iHop and ordered pancakes. Except for Manny, who got an omelette and coffee. Our waitress, a woman in her thirties with the hair and wrinkles of a woman in her sixties, nearly hyperventilated taking his order.

Before drinking, Manny filled his coffee with a powder, "full of good fats and collagen peptides and salt."

"I drink my coffee black," I said. "Like Abraham Lincoln did."

"Mine taste delicious. How is yours?" said Manny.

"Tastes terrible, as it ought."

"Burn more fat, *mi amigo grande*, and maybe you get a girlfriend."

Carlos ate a single bite of pancake and set his fork heavily down. Too antsy to eat. "Isabella. She is near?"

I said, "Probably. Within twenty miles. The only thing we know for certain, we are surrounded by sources of information."

"Why do we sit here?"

Manny said, "It is only eight. Quarter past eight."

"We're giving pimps time to rent rooms and run out their girls," I said.

"*Jesucristo*. You say Isabella, she is not working yet?"

"No way. Not yet." I set my mug of coffee onto the saucer and neatly cut my pancakes into bite sized squares.

"Then...what do we do?"

"We ask the pimps for directions."

"The pimps, they buy girls from Méjico? From the coyotes?" asked Carlos.

Manny shook his head, made a "Nuh-uh" sound, and ate his omelette.

"Most likely the local prostitution business is completely separate from the coyote extortion business," I explained. "We don't know who the coyote is. Or where he is. And the pimps, they don't know either. But if we hit a pimp hard enough, he'll point us to his boss. Then we go visit the boss. The boss won't be involved with coyotes, but he'll know guys who are. Then we go visit those guys, and so forth."

Carlos nodded his head, like carefully translating my modus operandi. "Follow the trail?"

"Yes. Working our way up the ladder."

"*Rápido*," said Manny.

"Manny and I used this technique in Los Angeles. Get high enough in the food chain, the guys know each other. Gotta work fast, though. We're going to piss off some powerful men. We don't want to be here long, and we don't want them to know who we are, and we don't want the coyote getting a warning. We want to be shoving a pistol up his nose just a few hours after we start. Get me?"

Carlos nodded. He set his head down on the table and said, "*Jesucristo*," again.

Manny looked at me over his mug. "Carlos be a wild bull tonight. He gonna kill everyone."

WE SAT in my Accord in a damp alley across from a nondescript motel, The Oceanside Inn. One of those dumps owned locally, not by a chain. Most of the lights within the big sign were burnt out; so were the sconces. Paper bags from three fast food joints sat wetly in the parking lot, cats prowled the exterior black iron staircase, and the blue light of a television flickered inside the walk-up front office.

But free cable!

From our vantage we could see each motel room door, all twenty-four of them. A Chevy Tahoe from the 1700's pulled in. The driver spoke with the front office, went back to the Tahoe, and three girls got out. One went into 203 by herself, and two went into 205. Just a guess, the girls were mid-twenties.

Manny got out with white electrical tape to disguise my license plate. Crouched at the rear.

In the back, Carlos began jacking shells into a pump-action twelve gauge shotgun, painted camouflaged.

"Carlos, the shotgun," I said. "It won't be necessary."

"Por que?"

"These guys are low level. They know next to nothing. And if you shoot them we gotta call the whole night off."

"But...my daughter."

"I know. Maybe you wait here," I said.

"I talk to those *pendejos*," he said. "But the shotgun will stay."

Within twenty minutes two cars had pulled up and an indistinct man went into each motel room. First customers of the night.

Manny, Carlos, and I got out of my Honda Accord, our three doors opening in unison. We didn't even plan it—you can't teach preternatural bravura.

The driver in the Tahoe didn't notice us until I knocked on the window. It was dark and the only things I saw inside were illuminated by the light of his phone. He was scrolling through pornography when I knocked.

The guy jumped. Strong kid, maybe twenty-five. His head was buzzed, skin pockmarked, and his hands were tattooed. He was by himself. Gun on the passenger seat.

The kid watched me. Watched Manny beside me. Started taking deep breaths. He didn't buzz the window down.

"Easy," I said. "We're not here for you."

"Take a walk," he told me through the window.

"After you give me some information, we're gone," I said. "No one gets hurt."

His words were muffled. "Information? Who the hell are you? Get out of here."

On the other side of the Tahoe, Carlos shoved both hands into the passenger door. Hard enough to scare the hell out of the driver, and hard enough to rock the car.

"Jesus," said the driver. His hand started pawing the passenger seat, searching for his gun. "What do you want?"

Manny casually removed his .357 and placed the muzzle flat against the window. The kid's eyes went wider.

I said, "Relax. Don't be an idiot. Don't go for a gun. We're all walking away. Understand? I want to talk to your boss."

"My boss?"

"Your boss."

"The hell?"

I nodded encouragingly.

"Yeah that guy."

Carlos hit the Tahoe again. Guy inside flinched.

"Man, get out of here!" he shouted. "I ain't doing anything wrong!"

"You start the car, we break both windows and haul you out," I explained.

"What do you want with my boss?"

"I want to know his name and his location. And I want to talk to him. I'll never mention you. Scout's honor," I said.

"You tryna get me killed? That it? I can't tell you nothing, buncha motherfuckers."

Behind us, one of the motel doors opened. Weak light spilled out and a man hurried to the stairs. He was kind of hopping and working at his belt.

"Johnny! Johnny!" called the woman, stalking out after him. She wore a little black skirt and a stained wife-beater t-shirt. No shoes. "Johnny he ain't paying!"

The guy hurrying down the steps shouted at no one in particular, "No, I...please...I changed my mind! This...this isn't...not what I thought..."

"Johnny he's leaving! He ain't even pay me!" She was shouting in a screech.

I pointed my finger at the guy in the Tahoe. "Don't move, Johnny."

"This is where I work!" he shouted through the window. "That asshole is skipping payment!"

Manny tapped the glass with his .357 and said, "Stay, mi amigo."

When the guy who was fleeing reached the bottom of the stairs, Manny was there. The man—early thirties, trim, meek-looking guy, maybe an accountant—pulled up short. Manny wrapped an arm around his neck. Kinda friendly, but also kinda like a headlock. He still held the pistol and it laid against the man's chest.

Manny said, "Señor, you pay the girl?"

"What, no...I...we didn't...I mean..."

"No? Yes?"

The guy gulped. "Nothing happened...I mean, you know...not like it should."

The girl on the balcony kept going, hard on the ears. "Little prick got his money's worth. *Believe* me. And he ain't pay. Johnny, you hear me?"

Johnny glared at me, unable to get out of his Tahoe, me on one side and Carlos on the other.

I smiled back.

"But..." the meek guy told Manny at the bottom of the black iron staircase. He was pale. Staring at the unexpected audience. "I mean, it happened...you know, so fast, and—"

"This your first time?" asked Manny.

"Are you...what, are you the...what's going on?"

"The girl upstairs, she is a lady," explained Manny. "And you made the arrangement. Sí? You go pay the lady."

The guy's face was only an inch or two from Manny's, and he experienced what we all did—that Manuel Martinez was absurdly good to look at, and that the attractive facade hid an animal. A dark and dangerous one.

Manny was frightening. Something like kinetic violence on the cusp.

"...um..." said the guy.

Manny turned him in a circle and pushed him back up the stairs. "Go. Now. Or I sodomize you with my pistol."

"Oh my god," said the man, jogging back up the stairs. "This...this whole thing...this is messed up."

Manny turned to me. "Mack, you hear? Sodomize? Good, yes?"

"Yeah real nice."

Carlos slammed his hands into the Tahoe again. "Open it. Open the door."

Johnny cursed.

I shook my head at Johnny. "Don't open it. His daughter's missing. He'll kill you."

"Oh god," said Johnny.

The man on the second floor threw some money at the girl. She cursed at him and lit a cigarette.

"Look at that, Johnny," I said. "He paid. We took care of your problem. How about that, Johnny?"

He groaned. Said, "Great. Real great."

"Last chance, Johnny," I said. "Before we come in there with you."

"Why you doing this, man?"

"You're low hanging fruit. Easy to get," I said. "But I'm not after you. I'm climbing my way up. Give me what I want and we're gone."

The trim and meek accountant carefully edged around Manny, ran to his Corolla, fumbled the keys, got inside, cursed loudly, started it, and left in a hurry.

"You're looking for Luigi," Johnny told me. Some would call his tone begrudging. "Luigi. In Willough, on 1st View."

"Luigi," I repeated. "1st View."

The girl at the railing leaned over. Took a long drag on her cigarette and waved at Manny. She propped up her breasts with her elbows. "Hey. Hey gorgeous. You coming up or what."

Manny blew her a kiss. "I cannot. But you, señorita, I will remember you tonight. When I sleep."

She snorted. "Lotta good does me now." All her weight was on the flimsy railing, tilted near the breaking point.

"Who says romance is dead?" I asked Johnny. "Luigi on 1st View. Give me more."

"Near the corner of Maple. There's an apartment building and a house. He rents rooms. Okay? Don't mention me. Now fuck off."

"Johnny, you know what's gonna happen if there's no Luigi there?" I said.

"Whatever man."

"You know what happens if you warn Luigi? We're coming back. And Carlos breaks your face."

He nodded without looking at me. "Okay okay. You think I'd tell Luigi I ratted on him? Get out of here, already."

"And I'm going to poke you in the ribs. A lot, Johnny. Until it's not fun anymore. You know what I'm talking about? When it's frustrating and a little painful? You're still laughing but you wish you weren't? You know, Johnny?"

Carlos gave me a look. Like he was rethinking his selection for sophisticated investigator.

"What?" I said. "It hurts when people poke you."

I made a *Let's go* motion by waving my finger in the air. Manny, Carlos, and I walked back to the Accord.

Johnny cursed again, the potty mouth.

4

Twenty minutes later we rolled through the intersection at 1st View and Maple, home of dilapidated multi-family houses. Even in the dark it didn't take a keen intellect to pick out Luigi's. Two girls slouched out front, leaning against a green Kia and smoking cigarettes. A guy sat on the concrete steps of what used to be a large house—two stories, pale blue vinyl siding, window air conditioners—but it was now broken into four rental units. Smart money was that Luigi rented all four. The guy on the steps smoked too, bent over his phone.

I buzzed the window down.

One of the girls—she had a smallish face and thin blonde hair and acne—called, "Park over there, baby. Is it your birthday or something?"

"Or something," I said.

"How many you got?"

"Just me."

"Come on out, baby. I'm your new girlfriend."

I opened the door and got out. Manny eased the Accord

up the gravel driveway and quietly motored behind the house.

The night air stank of cigarettes and sour liquor and sewage. It was quiet, nearby citizens having bolted their doors against the acknowledged hedonism taking place on 1st View.

"Well, damn, you're a big guy," the blonde said and she drew hard enough on her cigarette to use up half the tobacco.

She wore jean shorts, the kind with an elastic waist and drawstrings, and heels and a white sports bralette. She had holes in her nose and earlobes but no jewelry.

"How many girls you got inside?" I asked.

"That depends, baby. How many you need? I can be a jealous girlfriend, though."

The other girl leaning against the Kia never looked up. She had a phone in one hand and a cigarette in the other.

I said, "Luigi let me have as many as I want?"

"Sweetie, you got the cash? You can buy it all."

"That's swell. What a swell guy, that Luigi."

She made kind of a laugh through her nose. Her sinuses rattled. "Yeah, you know Luigi, a real Valentine."

"You do back scratches?"

"Back scratches? Sure baby. Whatever."

"Scalp massage?" I asked.

"You're kind of a weirdo, mister. What's your name?"

"Garfield. What's yours?"

"Jazzy."

"What about deep tissue, Jazzy? You know, harder than Swedish? Acupuncture? Hot rocks?"

"Garfield, we're wasting time, baby," she said.

"You like living here, Jazzy?"

"Sure. Paradise," she said.

"Where are you from?"

"Where should I be from?"

I said, "I'm from Richmond."

"How about that. Me too. No kidding," she said.

"You're a *liar*."

She didn't want to smile but she did. Her teeth were yellow and she was missing one on the bottom. "C'mon, big guy. Stop asking dumb questions. Let's go inside, yeah?"

"I can't," I said. "I'm here to see Luigi."

"This a joke? You wasting my time?"

"Luigi handles all the girls around here, right? Kinda like the pimp boss?"

I removed a big bill from my pocket and gave it to her.

"Oh," she said. "Oh shit. Go ahead talk to Luigi. He's on the stairs."

"No he's not," I said.

She turned. The motion stirred the air and her body produced an unwashed odor. "Yeah, he's...where'd Luigi go?" She pointed at the empty stairs. "He was right there, I swear."

"I'll bring him back in a couple minutes."

Jazzy stared after me but didn't follow as I went around back, stumbling a little in the dark.

Manny and Carlos were beating the hell out of Luigi in the shadow of an old Cadillac Escalade. I got there in time to see Carlos kick him in the mouth hard enough to loosen his teeth.

I got between Carlos and Luigi, who was on the gravel, holding his side and spitting blood. It was dark behind the house, no source of direct light. Luigi's shirt and pants were black.

"Enough," I told them. "Ease up."

"Luigi think he's tough," said Manny. "Pull a knife when I say we only want to talk. I tell him put it back. He didn't."

Carlos's chest was heaving.

Luigi raised up enough to spit a spray of blood our way. We stepped backwards and the mist landed on his own face. "Fuck you!"

"Oh yeah?" I said.

"Yeah, all yous. You think I don't got friends nearby? You think they won't be here soon?"

I couldn't see him well. But his accent sounded like New Jersey, one of those guys who say "Fugetaboutid" because they think they're supposed to.

"Luigi, we're just leaving," I said. "Before we go, I need to know the name of your boss."

"Yeah you can go straight to hell, you can, pal. I got ten guys I'm paying, all them drill you good."

"Sorry about your mouth. My friends get jumpy."

"Your friends get dead, when I'm through," said Luigi.

"Credit where it's due, Luigi. It's hard to act tough while cowering like a turtle in the gravel and cigarette butts. But you've managed it. Bravo. Who covers this area? Some guy out of Richmond? Out of DC?"

"Christ almighty, you're all dead."

"We're looking for a coyote," I explained helpfully.

"Coyote? What do I look like, a spic? What do I know about coyotes?"

"Luigi, the next five minutes will be a lot more pleasant if you spill the beans."

He laughed. I had enough light to see his teeth were red. "What are you gonna do? Your boyfriends already beat me up. Gonna beat me up some more? Go ahead." He said it like, "Ga'head."

Manny knelt at Luigi's feet. There was a snap-click, and

then another snap-click. Luigi glanced down, dismayed. His ankle had been handcuffed to the hitch of the old Cadillac Escalade.

"The hell?" he said. "You gonna drag me around town? Jesus."

"No," I said. "We're not."

He struggled but Manny and Carlos were stronger. Soon Luigi's right wrist was handcuffed to the bumper of my Honda Accord. He was stretched tight between the two vehicles.

"Okay," he said and gulped. "Okay, boys, let's be cool. Aight, got'damn it, let's relax. Okay?"

Watching this made my stomach churn.

Manny got behind the wheel of the Accord. Started the engine.

"Alright alright!" shouted Luigi. He thrashed helplessly. His eyes turned to me. He shouted over the motor roar. "Alright! Tell your boy to kill the engine!"

"My friend's crazy," I said and I shrugged like—what are you gonna do?

"Okay, okay!"

"You don't work with coyotes?" I asked.

"No!"

"Whose territory is this?" I asked.

Manny dropped the car into gear.

Luigi shouted, "Tito! His name's Tito!"

The Accord reversed a single inch, stretching Luigi further.

I made a throat slashing gesture at Manny. The car turned off.

Luigi was gasping. In the process of peeing his pants.

"Tito," I said.

Luigi nodded and started to cry.

"Tito?" said Carlos. "I know Tito."

"See?" whimpered Luigi, still stretched tight. "The spic knows him. Let me go, okay?"

"I don't know Tito. I'm getting confused with all the names," I said. "Who's Tito?"

Carlos said, "Tito. He works for Duane."

"Yeah! Yeah that's the guy! I heard'a Duane! Take off the cuffs, huh?"

"How come none of the crime bosses are women?" I wondered. "Perhaps the underworld is supercilious and sexist."

Manny snickered.

I knelt beside Luigi. "You promise not to warn Tito that we're on the way?"

"Yeah man, I swear. I swear to God."

"Luigi, are you lying?"

"No! No, honest! Who the hell are you guys? I swear."

Manny inserted his key into the cuffs and released Luigi's ankle.

"We're the good guys," I said. "Though it doesn't feel that way at the moment."

5

Sixty minutes after we'd first knocked on the Chevy Tahoe's window, Manny parked my Accord at a 7-11. It wasn't eleven p.m. yet. We were making good time.

"You two guys," said Carlos. "I work with Marcus. His crew act tough. Do tough things. But you two? You two *loco*."

Manny grinned. "Yeah, migo, that be inspired. Right, Mack? Inspired, I say. I almost hit the gas, just to see."

"That's disturbing, Manny," I said.

"Not disturbed. Inspired."

Carlos asked, "Now what?"

"Tell me about Tito."

"Tito, he is like Marcus. He run Virginia Beach and Norfolk, the way Marcus run Roanoke."

"What's he into?"

"*No lo sé.* Usual stuff. Drugs. Gambling. Guns. Girls. Money loaning."

"Lending," I said.

"Que?"

"A loan is a noun. It's a thing. Not a verb. You meant to say lending."

"But we call it loan shark, yes?" said Carlos.

Manny sighed. "Señor August, maybe teach English later."

I said, "We're the good guys. It's important we use the King's English. Instead of 'money lending,' Carlos, you could say 'usury' and impress your friends."

Manny and Carlos, from Puerto Rico and Mexico respectively, expressed a shared sentiment of feeling underwhelmed with my whiteness.

"This Tito," I said. "He a reasonable guy?"

"Not like Marcus. I don't mess with Tito."

"Then I think we'll call Duane."

"*Jesucristo*," said Carlos.

"I've met Duane. Talks soft, wears tight clothes to show off his muscles. I took a lot of money from him in a poker game, about a year ago. Maybe I won't mention my name."

"Good idea," said Manny. "White people hate you."

"Can you get me Duane's number?" I asked.

"*Simon*," said Carlos and he started texting.

While we waited for a response, Manny went inside for a cherry Slurpee and coffees. Light rain began pattering on the windshield.

Carlos said, "At Luigi's house. Those two girls you talk to? They were eighteen?"

"Probably not. It was close."

"What do we do? They are kids."

I turned in my seat to look at him.

"You're a professional criminal, Carlos. You've seen underaged girls before."

"Sí. Sí, I know. But..."

"Somehow the world changes when it could be your kid."

Carlos ducked his head. Twisted a shotgun shell over and over in his thick fingers. I turned back, facing forward.

"Sí," he said in a soft voice. "The world changes. Why does the police not stop them?"

"There are hundreds of strip motels," I said. "Bust one, Luigi will start the racket at two others. Not enough police, not enough money, and dozens of Luigis waiting to make money, plus a thousand lost girls. The improprieties of the world outstrip our funds."

Manny returned with his Slurpee and coffees. The lady working the register gaped after him, like she'd seen a ghost. The Ghost of Christmas Gorgeous.

After a moment, Carlos said, "But they are teenagers. The police, they should do something."

I said, "Why the police? Why not you? You live in that world, Carlos."

"Me?"

"Yeah, why's it gotta be the police?" I asked.

"They are police. It is their job."

"But you're a human. And a father," I said. "It's our job. Collectively."

"But we drove away. We left."

Manny drank his red goo and grinned. "Don't let him fool you, Carlos. Señor Mack is writing down all the addresses and license plates. After this be over, he will call social services and then the police. He cannot sit still and do nothing."

Carlos leaned forward, so his head was closer to ours. "You are?"

I shrugged. "Don't tell anyone. My heart of gold could ruin business."

"Why do you not call police now?" asked Carlos.

"Mack, he does not trust the government," said Manny.

"He like to spook people and let them make the right choice. He hoping Luigi gets scared straight. Those two girls run home or something."

"I do not understand."

"Cleaning yourself up," I said, "is nothing the government can coerce its citizens to do with any efficiency. The government should be used only as a last resort."

"Say that again," said Carlos. "But different."

"It's impossible to fix someone. They gotta decide to fix themselves. Once the police arrest them, the girls will dig in their heels. Resist. Because that's all they know how to do. Much better if they come to their own conclusions. So maybe Luigi quits because we almost tore his arms off. Maybe he sees the light. Gives his girls a ride somewhere healthy. Probably not, but it's the best I can do. We scare them and give them the chance. A reminder they at least have a choice. Freedom is a terrible thing, but it's the best path to independence and healthy interdependence."

"My daughter, Isabella. She does not have a choice. She was taken."

"Why we're here with guns," I said.

Carlos's phone beeped softly.

"Okay. I have the number. Phone number for Duane." He didn't sound happy about it.

Manny reached into his 7-11 bag and pulled out one of those cheap burner phones with a temporary number. I powered it on and got the number and dialed it.

It rang twice.

A voice came on. "Yeah."

"Talk to Duane," I said. "Pretty please."

"What about."

"He's been nominated for Villain of the Year. I'm on the awards committee."

In the back seat, Carlos groaned. Manny grinned around his straw.

The line stayed silent.

I said, "I'd like to speak to Duane about a complex situation involving Tito and Marcus Morgan."

He didn't respond but the shade of silence changed. There came faint sounds of movement. A minute later, I heard music.

A new voice. "It's late. Who is this?"

"Hello Duane. I represent one of your underlings," I said. "Let's call him John Wick. John Wick is several rungs below you on the ladder of villainy."

"One of my underlings."

"He's an associate of Marcus Morgan, though Marcus doesn't know about this particular quandary."

"This is a weird fucking phone call," he said. He spoke in a soft rasp. Power in abeyance.

"John Wick's daughter is being held by a coyote working in your area."

"How do you know the coyote is working in my area?" asked Duane.

"He demanded PayPal. We refused and requested a cash drop. He told us the cash drop was in Virginia Beach, and so was the girl."

"Yeah, so? Big deal, we do that," said Duane. "Part of the business. Tell John Wick to pay the promised money and he gets his daughter."

"Trouble is, John Wick is now being extorted. The coyote is holding the girl hostage. He's demanded four times the agreed price. We're now in Virginia Beach, here to kill the coyote," I said. "I figured it's your area, we owe you the respect of calling first."

Duane stayed quiet. I heard him breathing. Carlos's

breathing was inaudible, if it existed at the moment.

"You're right to contact me," said Duane. "I appreciate the respect. I mean that."

"You bet."

"Who is this, again?"

"I never said."

"You never said. Okay, Never Said. Four times the agreed amount?" he asked.

"That's right."

"We don't kidnap little girls and extort the parents."

"I figured," I said.

"You figured."

"Now we're worried about the coyote being, ahhh, criminally corrupt. We're worried he might kill the girl after getting the money," I said. "Which is why we brought guns."

"We don't kill little girls."

"A rogue coyote might."

"Yeah. You and John Wick, you brought guns. You don't make a move yet. I'll contact you again at this number," he said. "You understand?"

"Your instructions are limpid. We can wait a little while."

"Limpid," he said and he hung up.

I lowered the phone.

Carlos released a big blast of air.

Manny said, "You got that smooth way of talking, Mack. I was a criminal boss? I be terrified of you."

"But," I said. "Do you think limpid was over the top?"

"Dunno. What's it mean?"

"I forget." I looked at my steaming styrofoam cup. "Did you put your fancy milk in my coffee?"

"No."

"Manny."

"I put only heavy cream and stevia and some keto

powder. I keep packets in my pocket," he said. "Makes it healthy."

In the back, Carlos sipped his. Made a happy noise. "Manuel, *café blanco*, it's good, migo, gracias."

I said, "I was a crime boss, I'd pour this witches brew in both your laps. Do you know how many carbs are in your red Slurpee?

"Don't judge. I having a cheat meal."

6

Duane called back after midnight.

I answered and he said, "Coyote you're after is named Angelo. Works with Tito out of Norfolk."

"We know Tito."

"You know Tito," he said. "You leave him out of this. You understand? This isn't because of Tito."

"I will cross him off my list. With *red* ink."

"Off your list," he said. "Good. Angelo is your guy. He's running a racket behind my back."

"I knew it. Criminally corrupt. The outrage," I said.

"You're a smart ass. I know you. You're the dick out of Roanoke."

"Nope," I said.

"Yes you are. I met you. Friends with Marcus Morgan."

"Nope," I said again. "Though that guy sounds swell and handsome. I am someone less witty, however."

"Whatever. Angelo operates out of Norfolk." He gave me an address. I repeated it and Manny wrote it down.

"You got a picture of Angelo you can text me?"

"No I don't got a fucking picture of Angelo I can text you," he said.

"Okay grumpy."

"You have help?"

"I have help."

"Go get John Wick's little girl. Angelo doesn't know you're coming. Do me a favor. You find Angelo, you put a hole in his head."

I scratched at my chin and whispered, "I will do you this favor."

"Godfather? You doing the godfather at me?"

"Heavens no. Thanks Duane. We're gonna go kill many of your underlings," I said.

"Only Angelo. You hear me?"

I said, "I don't know what he looks like, so we'll just shoot everyone," and I hung up.

Carlos smacked his hands together hard in the backseat. "*Vamanos!* Let's go, señor Mack! You got Isabella. She is there. It is time for my shotgun."

ONE IN THE MORNING.

We parked at an Asian massage parlor in Portsmouth, just across the Elizabeth River. The economy of Portsmouth was propped up on freight shipping, mountains of it. There was no new construction but this part of town looked heathy. Like, we have enough money but we don't want nice things because sailors might break them.

The parlor was sandwiched between a tattoo place and a sub shop. The three storefronts shared a damp parking lot in need of paving. The massage parlor was fronted with big windows, through which we could see those sit-down massage chairs with faded white padding. The lights were off but there was a glow in the rear, beyond a partition.

"Isabella, she is in there?"

"Maybe. In the basement," I said. "My guess, it's a massage parlor with a sex shop below."

Manny flashed his marshal badge. "We do this legal? Shoot some traffickers in the name of America?"

"Let's see how it goes. You make the call afterwards. Carlos and I were never here."

In the back, Carlos rocked back and forth, swaying the Honda.

I said, "I hope they don't shoot my car. I only got the windows replaced two months ago."

"If we gotta run outside and hide behind your car, our troubles be bigger than your windows," Manny said.

"There are not many cars here," noted Carlos.

"Most in the back. But I'd prefer not to use that ingress. I wanna surprise the guard."

Manny checked his pistol.

Carlos hoisted his twelve-gauge.

I got out of the Accord. The night was chilly and wet. Recently fried food was carried on the breeze. I carried the 1911 in my right hand, and I tucked a .38 special at the small of my back.

I saw myself in the reflection of the massage parlor windows. Of the three of us, I looked least impressive. Which, I thought, was a shame.

An unexpected gift—the front door was unlocked.

"Don't shoot anyone unless you have to. Let's go," I said.

The glass door opened smoothly. The front room was clean and warm and smelled like perfumed lotion. We moved quickly and without sound. Beyond the first partition we found curtained rooms with massage tables. Rows of neatly folded white towels. Oriental pictures and incense sticks. We kept moving towards the far glow.

At the rear exit, there was a stairwell leading below. A giant stood there. A giant in khakis and a dark blue sports jacket. He was bigger than me, which is hard. He didn't hear our approach.

Carlos fired his twelve-gauge, an explosion of sound. Like the world blew up. The giant was caught in the chest and knocked backwards into the wall.

"*Jesú*, Carlos, my ears," said Manny. It was hard to hear over the ringing in my head.

"There goes our surprise."

"What?"

Despite my tinnitus, I became aware of screaming below. The noise came up the stairwell.

I knelt beside the giant, who was coughing. I fumbled in his jacket for his gun: a black 9. I stuffed it in my pocket.

His stomach was rock hard. I smacked it.

"You wear a flack vest? Smart giant," I said, possibly too loud.

He coughed some more, fumbling where the shot had nearly broken the vest.

"Dammit," he groaned.

"Stay put and you get to live," I told him.

Carlos leapt down the stairs.

He shouted, "Isabella! Dónde estás, bebé? Soy aquí!"

The basement walls were painted cinderblock and the floor was a hard flecked vinyl. The ceiling was low, nearly touching my head. I had to duck under the fluorescent housings. The space felt small, most of it dedicated to little rooms created by temporary curtain dividers.

The guilty parties were hiding from Carlos's bazooka

behind the curtains, the scene momentarily frozen and silent.

"Everyone out," I said. "You gotta run. Police will be here soon."

Half-naked women ran out from the curtained partitions, crying. They ran deeper into the basement. Half-naked men emerged, hopping into their pants and bolting up the stairs. The women were Caucasian and Hispanic and Asian. The men were all fat white guys.

"Angelo?" I asked. "Where is Angelo?"

A guard, a wiry Latino, got the drop behind us but he hesitated. Manny threw a left into his stomach and then crisply clipped him in the skull with his pistol. The kid folded and didn't get up.

I turned off the mp3 player, which had been pumping oriental meditation music through speakers on the wall.

Carlos raged. He called, "Isabella!" again and stalked deeper into the basement. Men and women alike went wide-eyed at his shotgun. He had lost the ability to reason.

There was a second guard, another thin Hispanic guy, hiding behind a support column. He desperately wanted to be elsewhere. He had a gun but didn't know what to do with it. I raised my pistol at him.

He dropped his and went onto his knees, eyes closed.

"No no! No dispares! Por favor!"

"Dónde está Angelo?" I said.

Where's Angelo?

Without opening his eyes he pointed farther in, towards the back corner where the women ran. There was a second half to the basement, hidden by a flimsy wooden paneling with a single door.

I called, "Angelo. Got a message from Duane. Come out and you can live."

From behind the door came a voice. "My friends! I come out, you don't shoot?"

Carlos took a step towards it. I held up my hand—wait.

"Come out, Angelo, and I won't shoot you," I said. "Duane sent us."

"What for?"

"Come out or we come in."

A man hesitantly slid into view. Good looking guy, curly thick black hair. He wore chinos and a white linen shirt, unbuttoned. No shoes.

"My friends!" he said, forcing a smile. "This can all be cleared up."

Carlos shouted, "Dondé está Isabella?"

Angelo shot him a second look. "Carlos?"

"And company," said Manny.

"You came all the way here, Carlos? I have her! No harm is done!" cried Angelo.

"She is here?"

"Yes! She is here! All is well, Carlos. Take her."

"Don't shoot him," I said.

From his hip, Carlos fired his twelve-gauge. Unlike the giant, who had rocked backwards, Angelo lost a chunk of his midsection. He spun and landed wetly.

Women screamed again. I considered doing the same.

"Isabella!" Carlos shouted and he barged through the door into the rooms beyond.

Manny and I stood over Angelo, whose fate was sealed but would suffer a few more minutes. Manny shot him neatly in the head to end it.

"I think maybe America and the marshal don't take credit for this one," he said.

7

Isabella was unharmed, though she looked like she'd had a miserable week. She slept with her head on her father's lap across the back seat. Carlos smiled at her for hours, stroking her brown hair. Eventually he also drifted off, surrendering to the Accord's faint drone.

Manny yawned. "What time Carlos hire you?"

"Three, maybe," I said, eating a doughnut procured from a Dunkin drive-thru. Chocolate glazed with sprinkles. "Three-thirty."

"You find the girl ten hours later. Now they safe and asleep and almost home. You be a wizard."

"Like Gandalf, I am."

"Who?"

"You need to read more high fantasy," I said. "We got lucky tonight. It could have been difficult."

"You'll call social services tomorrow? About the prostitutes?"

"Yeah. Might not do much good. You know what the state does with at-risk girls like that? Sends them to youth detention centers. Throws them in with horny boys."

Manny said, "That's not true. Can't be true."

"But it is." I glanced at his speedometer—he was doing ninety-four. Were we racing someone?

"Maybe me and you, Mack, we start an orphanage. M&M Orphanage, we call it."

"An orphanage run by two single men catering exclusively to young prostitutes?"

"Ah. I see the problem. This is why you are the brains of our orphanage, migo.

WE PULLED into our driveway at 5:30am, still an hour before the sky turned a weak and watery blue. Manny and I helped haul Carlos's stuff to his old gray pickup. He carried Isabella, who might not wake for a week.

I removed the envelope of cash from my pocket. Counted out a few bills and held the rest out for him.

"Pleasure doing business with you, Carlos. Keep me in mind for all your abduction needs," I said.

He held up his brawny hands.

"No, señor August. I paid you. That is yours. Fair and fair."

"Carlos, I don't charge exorbitant flat fees. I charge by the day. We worked for one day and that's what you paid me. The amount of money in this envelope is lunacy."

"I get you a diamond?"

"I don't know what that means," I said. "And I don't need one."

"But we got Isabella and I am very happy."

"As are all my clients."

He said, "It was dangerous. You could have died."

"Okay, good point." I slid out one more big bill. "Happy now? Take the rest."

Which he did. And then nearly killed Manny and me. Death by fierce embrace.

THE HOUSE WAS silent in the way that well-made homes were at 5am.

Manny went to go sleep a few hours in the guest room. Bunk with Fat Susie, maybe.

I laid down on the leather couch in the living room. Got under a blanket. Propped my head on a throw pillow.

There was a gorgeous blonde in my bedroom. And I was lonely. If I went in, I would start undressing her and she would let me.

But she wasn't mine and I wasn't hers. She was a prostitute. Still untangling herself as best she knew how.

People had to do these things themselves, in my opinion.

So.

I could wait.

8

Ronnie woke me two hours later. Fully clothed, the prude. She was on her knees by the couch and she stroked my hair. "Hello Mackenzie."

"Hello Ronnie," I said. As I did, she popped a breath mint into my mouth.

She said, "Don't get up. Was last night's excursion successful?"

"Twas."

"Carlos's daughter is home? You and the luscious Manny are unharmed?" she asked.

"We are great American heroes, yes."

"I knew you'd do it. My confidence in you borders on worship." She kissed my forehead. "Kix was a delight. We partied late into the eight o'clock hour. Your father and the Sheriff came home, so I released Reginald. Stackhouse was eyeballing him suspiciously, anyway."

"You mean Fat Susie."

"A very unflattering moniker."

"Thank you for watching Kix."

She smiled and kissed me again. On the nose.

"You owe me. But now I need to dash. The daughter of a local wealthy family snorted several lines of coke and crashed her BMW an hour ago. I'm off to see that justice isn't served. Aren't I the worst?"

"I like you anyway."

"You love me, you mean. Though it's complex as hell. But one day, Mackenzie, one day it won't be. I'll be free and clean and all yours," she said. She had lowered her mouth until her lips brushed mine with each plosive syllable. "And I will grant you your every wish."

"You're awfully suggestive for a babysitter. You weren't even my first choice."

"Ask me out soon, please," she said.

"Once you're single."

"I will be."

"Ronnie," I said.

"Yes Mackenzie."

"I'm going back to sleep. My son gets up in an hour."

"Yes Mackenzie. I'll be waiting by the phone."

KIX DID ME A SOLID, slept in thirty minutes later than usual. He was clearly not pleased that it was I greeting him instead of Ronnie. I brought him to the kitchen, eased him into his high chair, and gave him a bottle of milk.

He casually backhanded the bottle off the tray and arched an eyebrow at me.

I shrugged. "Your loss."

Fetch me the milk.

"You knocked the milk off. Purposefully."

Fetch me the milk, please.

"This is called natural consequences, son. Pain is good for you."

Fetch the milk, now.

I chopped up slices of banana and apple and set them on the tray. He pointed at the bottle and expressed his dismay. Then he flung the bits of fruit.

I sat on the chair across from him. Sipped my coffee and rubbed my grainy eyes. "Your aim is terrible, kid. You didn't hit me once."

What a nasty thing to say. I can barely operate my fingers independently.

"You're in no position to be flippantly flinging your food. Not only is it unkind, it's unwise."

Dad. Stop being heinous. Fetch the bottle. And I will throw it farther this time.

"Last night I bravely stormed the sinister gates of an immoral massage parlor and rescued a kidnaped little girl. Today, a one-year-old throws food at me and makes narcissistic demands."

Dad.

"Kix."

Please return my bottle. I'm growing hoarse.

"Do not throw it again or it's gone for good," I said. I picked the bottle up and set it on his tray.

He forehand smashed it across the room. Farther this time.

A WOMAN WAS WAITING outside my office door when I arrived at 9:20am. She wore expensive red slip-ons with petite wedge heels, black slacks, and a beige double-breasted peacoat. Underneath, a red turtleneck. Her hair was brown and long and soft, and when she saw me she smiled and it created multiple laugh lines around her eyes and the corners of her lips. A genuine leather satchel was slung over her shoulder. All in all, it was a good look.

"You have to be Mr. August," she said and she shivered. "I recognize the photo."

"Did you not for a moment wonder if I was Tom Hardy?"

"The guy who played Mad Max?" she asked. "I see the resemblance, I suppose."

"I knew it."

"You're late. Your office is scheduled to open at nine."

"I almost didn't come in today. How long would you have waited? It's chilly," I said, keen weatherman that I was.

"I have a thermos. And you haven't answered any of my messages. So, a while," she said. "Can we chat?"

I unlocked the stairwell door for her and we went up. She followed me into the office. The area wasn't especially cold but I turned on the space heater.

"I make a mean cup of Keurig," I offered.

"So can most recent law school grads and they're idiots. I brought my own, thanks. Help yourself though. I don't mind."

I pulled out a Yeti rambler from my own satchel. "I am as prepared as thou."

"You look exhausted."

"It was a harrowing night."

"Your office has an odor." She settled into my client chair, still wearing her peacoat and shivering inside it. "Smells like...a zoo, maybe?"

"Thank you. It's potpourri. I purchase masculine scents."

"Men should smell like zoos?"

I nodded. "The good ones."

"Is that a Bible on your shelf?"

I nodded again. "Read it?"

"Sure. We studied the greats in law school, which included Paul. He was a genius, you know. On the level with Plato."

"You'll have to enlighten me. His run-on sentences are cumbersome. You're an attorney?"

"I am. Candice Hamilton." She crossed her legs but her hands remained in the pockets of her coat. In the corner, the space heater made some noise. "I'm the girl who's been pestering you about Grady Huff."

"Grady Huff. Trust fund kid living at the lake, killed his cleaning lady," I said.

"That's the guy."

"Grady Huff is gonna swing."

"I'll have a heck of a time picking jurors who don't agree with you," she said. "In fact, that's why I had the trial moved to Roanoke. Extreme prejudice due to notoriety at the lake. We had no shot at twelve disinterested jurors."

I said, "Trial is in twenty-one days? Twenty-eight, something like that. Isn't it a little late to be hiring guys like me?"

"According to my local contacts, you're the only guy worth trusting. And I'm new to the case too. My client fired his entire defense team a week ago. He filed motion to withdraw counsel and they couldn't sign it fast enough."

"He's rough on his attorneys?"

"He's a deplorable, despicable, and irredeemable ass."

"Wow," I said. "Count me in."

"However, I recently sank fifty thousand dollars into a slam-dunk medical malpractice case and whiffed. Mr. Huff's deep pockets come at a good time."

"You motioned to get a later trial date?"

"My client refuses to waive his right to a speedy trail,"

said Candice Hamilton. "He's out of time. The trial is happening."

"Why won't he waive—"

"I told you. Because he's a deplorable, despicable—"

"And irredeemable ass. Got it."

"He cannot imagine losing. So why delay the victory," she said. "His words."

"Why did he hire you, a med mal lawyer?"

Her chin tilted upwards with a bit of defiance. "I am primarily defense. Some big wins under my belt. I once worked with Kenneth Starr on a death row case," she said.

"*The* Kenneth Starr?"

"After retiring from government work, Mr. Starr worked pro bono in Virginia on the Robin Lovitt case. I was part of local counsel. We lost. But still."

I said, "Grady Huff is gonna swing. All you do is lose."

"Those are two of my only losses. My record is quite good. And yes, he probably will."

"I don't want to help an irredeemable ass avoid the noose."

"It'll be a life sentence, not a noose. I can triple your daily rate," she said.

"Meh."

"Fine, quintuple. As I said, his pockets are deep."

I picked up my coffee and drank some. The space heater began to make its presence felt. "Didn't Grady Huff admit his guilt?"

She smiled. Despite it being a grim and exasperated smile, I enjoyed it. The laugh lines and dimples gave her face character. "Yes he did. Being a trust fund kid has a way of atrophying one's brain. I'm not trying to prove his innocence; he absolutely killed Juanita Yates, the young cleaning lady. I'm working on the motive and mindset angle."

"*Mens rea*," I said, displaying the uttermost limits of my defense knowledge.

She looked pleased I knew the term. "Precisely."

I used to be a police officer, I wanted to say.

Oh really? she would ask.

In Los Angeles, I would say.

Tell me more.

The homicide division, I would say.

And then she would swoon.

Almost certainly. Everyone knows defense lawyers love cops.

Instead I said, "No deal forthcoming from the DA?"

"The case has recently taken an unexpected turn. The federal government has gotten involved," she said.

"The heck you say."

"A big shot federal prosecutor arrived from Washington to be co-counsel. Any hope we had of a deal is off."

I replaced the Yeti mug onto the desk and laced my fingers across my stomach, which now felt hollow and queasy. "A federal prosecutor has inexplicably decided to sit in on this open-and-shut homicide case in Roanoke," I said.

"Yes."

"Would his name by chance be Darren Robbins?"

Her right leg, which had been kind of bouncing on top of her left, stopped. "In fact it is."

"He's on this case *pro hac vice*?"

"Right. Do you know him?"

Darren Robbins.

Corrupt prosecutor in the pocket of the District Kings.

Fiancé of Veronica Summers.

He pimped Ronnie out to his buddies. Trafficking her sexual services via blackmail.

Number one enemy of Mackenzie August.

I said, "I know of him."

"And?"

"A notable coward, an infinite and endless liar."

Candice Hamilton sat up straighter, hope springing eternal. "You're quoting something but I can't place it. So you'll help?"

"Help stick it to Darren Robbins? Absolutely."

"Considering it's known Grady killed her, we put his criminal intent on trial. Our goal is to reduce it from first-degree murder to voluntary manslaughter, or crime of passion. We do that, Darren Robbins goes home embarrassed, tail between his legs."

"Do you know where Darren is staying?"

"Hotel Roanoke, same as me," she said.

"Maybe I'll go beat him up until he leaves."

She laughed. A little hesitant. Probably to hide her arousal at my tough-guy act. "That wouldn't help my client much."

"Oh right, him. I forgot."

"I'm reading motions and briefs and deposition transcripts twelve hours a day. I need you to dig up something new. Anything. On either Grady Huff or the victim."

"Something that will indicate a crime of passion."

"Precisely."

I said, "How big is your crew?"

"Just me and a paralegal. My partners are bitter about losing the medical malpractice money, so I'm temporarily forsaken. Most likely until I cash Mr. Huff's final check."

"Well then. We've not a moment to lose."

9

I skipped lunch in favor of an hour nap in my chair.

In China it's a cultural right to nap during work. Keeps the brain healthy. And those people seem really well adjusted and friendly.

I slept fitfully with disorienting dreams and I woke feeling no better. Maybe grouchier.

The Chinese know nothing, those communists.

The drive to the Western Virginia Regional Jail was not a pleasant one. First one must suffer through the worst part of Salem, clotted with stoplights and chain restaurants and car washes and loan shops on Route 11. After that the population thins out but it's ugly country, even more so in the rain. The jail is hidden by scrubby woods off an unmarked country lane. Closer up to the ugly brick rupture of a building, the landscape is uneven grass and broken pavement. I parked and watched the drizzle and wondered if it was too late for my dream of playing centerfield in the majors.

Probably.

I went inside. One of the deputies at the first security point recognized me but he made me check my gun anyway.

The beefy deputy leered. "Hey Mack. I heard you was dating the Sheriff."

"Never listen to gossip. It'll rot your ears."

"So, are you?"

I asked, "Would it make you respect me more if I was?"

"Hell yeah. She's grade A, you know it."

I debated admitting she was dating my father and not me. Not sure that would help business.

I said, "I am not romantically intertwined with your boss. But if you think Stackhouse is lovely, you should see my babysitter."

His mouth dropped an inch and he scrutinized me with one eye half-closed. "Oh?"

I said, "She's the goddess on whom these airs attend."

He buzzed open the security door.

"God, I forgot how stupid you talk," he said.

The conference room was concrete and cinderblock and body odor. An attorney fidgeting in the corner, rearranging his cheap suit and tie, waiting for a client to appear. He had the look of a man fresh off an online law degree, making a go at being an attorney in his late forties and regretting his life choices.

A second beefy deputy walked in. This guy looked even angrier than the cop at the security checkpoint. Buzzcut, swollen neck, perpetual frowny-face. As long as we have prisons, there will be abuse. You cannot give angry men on steroids with superiority complexes power over helpless men in shackles and expect harmony. I liked most cops, but jails had a way of souring even the most valiant heart.

Grady Huff slouched in behind the guy. Grady could have been thirty, he could have been fifty. Balding with a bad combover. Untidy facial hair that highlighted his fat jowls instead of camouflaging them. Big head, small face, lazy expression. Walked like he had flat duck feet.

"Ah Christ, he's not a girl," said Grady. Then he laughed, a forced croak. "I thought you brought me some ass."

The deputy didn't bother looking at him. He left.

Grady held up his hands, which were cuffed.

"Hey, Goliath. How about you request these be taken off, huh?"

"Nah," I said. "Better safe than sorry."

"What, you're scared? First time in a prison, fatty?"

"Terrified. Petrified. Of you. And your apparent ability to eat anything."

"Are you poor? You look poor." He sat at the table with me. But he sat on the opposite side, two seats down. The act of moving made him wheeze. "Where's Candice?"

"Your attorney will not be joining us today."

"God, the mouth on that bitch. Right? I told her I'll give her ten grand for a conjugal visit." He winked at me because we were both studs and knew the secret code of how to talk about women. Just us two guys, shooting the breeze, we were. "She said no. Like she's Mother Teresa or some shit."

"I'm Mackenzie. I'm helping get your sentence reduced."

"Try again, *fatty*. You mean you're getting the charges *dropped*," he said. He issued flecks of spittle when he pronounced the F in fatty.

"You confessed to murder. And confessed it to half a dozen people. Including the police."

"So what. Bitch deserved it. Do you know where I went to school?" he said.

"My guess, a culinary school. But you were the taste tester."

"Episcopal High, in *Alexandria*. You probably never

heard of it, buried in some sweaty city school. It's *elite*." He laughed again, the same contrived croak.

"Wow," I said.

"That's right, wow. Episcopal High. Private boarding school."

"We'll tell the jury that. Case dismissed."

"Don't be an ass. I can't go in front of a jury," he said with a scoff.

"They'd love you, Grady. A real winner."

"Jurors are *poor*. They'd hate me because I got money. Why the *hell* do we let people like them judge people like me."

"You mean, dropouts."

He wiped his mouth. "Huh?"

"You didn't finish high school. I read your file."

"I own a stake in Pepsi. *Pepsi*. Fatties like you making me rich. I don't need a high school diploma."

"Do you like your cell?" I asked.

"What do you think, jackass." Another laugh.

I super hated that sound.

"You're going to be in it for the next forty years. Maybe longer," I said.

"Don't be an ass. I hired Candice."

"Doesn't matter."

"Doesn't matter? The internet says she's a big deal."

"You could hire Gandhi, but with two weeks to go you'd still get life in prison."

"Do you know how much money gets deposited into my checking account? *Every* month?"

"Tell me about the girl you murdered," I said.

"Two hundred thousand dollars, motherfucker. Fatties at Taco Bell drinking Pepsi."

"Juanita Yates."

He stopped. Leaned backwards on the bench. Set his hands on the table with a clink. "Yeah? So?"

"Tell me about her."

"I shot her with a gun," he said.

"What kind?"

"What?" he said.

"The gun, what kind of gun, you nincompoop."

"I dunno. The wild west kind."

"A revolver," I guessed.

"The kind with the spinning wheel thing."

"How'd you get a gun?"

"Anyone can get a gun. Took me four whole minutes."

"Why'd you shoot Juanita Yates?"

"Bitch deserved it," he said.

"Why?"

"Just did, fatty."

"How long had she been working for you?"

"Who cares," he said.

"The jury will."

"I'm not talking to a jury."

I said, "You were in love with Juanita?"

He paused, half a second. "Don't be an idiot."

"I found her photo. She was kinda cute."

"Kinda? Fatty like you wishes, kinda."

"She was more than kinda cute?" I asked.

"Who cares. She was the *cleaning* lady."

"So?"

"God you're dumb. She's a maid."

"So?" I said again. "A cute one."

"I called her Nita. Couldn't pronounce her real name. One of those stupid Mexican names."

"You and Nita were in love."

"Stop...seriously, you're a stupid idiot, know that? Maybe she was in love with *me*."

"I bet she was."

"Of course she was. But it wasn't the other way round."

"You didn't reciprocate her affection," I said.

"Exactly, genius. Genius fatty."

"Did Nita have a family?"

"No, she was alone, like me. I mean, I guess. I have no idea."

"Which is it? She was alone? Or you have no idea?" I asked.

"I said I have no idea if she had family, fatty."

"How much do you weigh?"

"How much...I don't know. One eighty."

"Grady Huff," I said. "Your left leg weighs more than one eighty."

"I wasn't screwing the maid," he said. "She wanted to screw *me*, that's a different story. Guys like me, guys with money, we got friends and girls *forever*. I didn't need her."

The attorney in the corner was packing up, realizing his client didn't want to see him. Poor guys, both of them. He was openly eavesdropping into our conversation. My nonpareil Socratic questioning poleaxed him. I assumed.

"Did you let her?" I said.

Grady asked, "Let her what?"

"Juanita wanted to screw you; did you let her?"

"I guess, maybe, I dunno."

"Of course you did. Rich guy like you, cute girl like her, why not? No harm in that."

He nodded, like this made sense. "Yeah. No harm. I let her. For months I let her."

"What'd her mom think of you?" I asked.

"Her mom's dead."

"You said you didn't know—"

"I *think* her mom's dead. I forget. I have no idea."

"Nowhere on any police report I read this afternoon does it mention you and Nita were romantically entangled. But I think you were," I said.

"I didn't say romance. I said, I let her screw me. Cause I'm a nice guy. Fatty."

"Why didn't you admit this to the police?"

"I got a reputation, you know? Guys like me, we're rich. We kill people whenever we want. That's what my friends do. Might look bad, me and the cleaning lady screwing. You can't tell anyone, right? This is confidential?"

"So killing someone gives you credibility with your friends. But bonking the maid doesn't?"

"Something like that. I mean, bonking the maid is fine. But...you'd have to go to a boarding school like *Episcopal High* to get it."

"Falling in love with her would definitely crush your reputation," I said.

He laughed, the wheezing croak. "Obviously, fatty. No one does that."

"Obviously."

He insulted me a while longer and then I left. Despite his best efforts I'd learned a lot. On the way out I stopped at the security desk.

The deputy asked, "How'd it go with Mr. Sunshine?"

"He thinks I'm fat."

"He says I'm retarded. His words. Not sure which is worse."

"Yours is worse. I can diet," I said.

"Yours is worse. I can read a book."

"But can you?" I asked. "You should tell him that word is deeply offensive now."

"Sure I will."

"How many visitors has he received?" I asked.

"Guess."

"None."

"Correct. No letters and no packages either," said the deputy.

"Poor Grady Huff."

"Yeah my heart is breaking for him."

DRIVING BACK to Roanoke I called Marcus Morgan, Local mobster and Episcopalian.

"August," he said, speaking in a deep rumble.

"Morgan," I said, dropping my voice to match his. "What are you wearing?"

"Not a smile, at the moment."

"Are you beating someone up? Shoveling cocaine into baggies? Laughing maniacally? Stroking a hairless cat? Insulting James Bond? Building a huge laser?"

"Right now I be listening to a moron," he said. As soon as I hung up, he would laugh a lot at my jokes. I assumed.

"Why is Fat Susie walking around with Ronnie?" I asked.

"Work stuff."

"I need details."

"Why? Are you her boyfriend? No you ain't. Do you work for me? No you don't," he said.

"Did you know Fat Susie's real name is Reginald?"

"I did."

"I'm going to ring your doorbell repeatedly until you tell me why he's following Ronnie around," I said.

"A buyer approached Veronica Summers about purchasing Calvin's fields of pot. And about purchasing his contracts. Your girl Ronnie, she said no. Ruffled a few feathers in Washington. So I let her take Fat Susie until it gets straightened out."

"Why'd she refuse the offer?"

"Hafta ask her," he said.

"Does Fat Susie's presence have anything to do with Darren Robbins, the powerful mobster lawyer goon?"

"Maybe."

"Did you know he's in town?" I asked.

"I did know that."

"Does Ronnie know?"

"She does know that," he said.

"Do you know what Carlos meant when he offered me a diamond?"

"I do know what he meant by a diamond, yes. It's work jargon."

"Why does no one tell me anything."

"Know what you are? An intrusive pain in the ass."

"Will Fat Susie kill Darren on sight?" I asked.

"Course not. You and Darren gonna have it out, one of these days, huh," he said. "Hope I'm there to watch. Guess who called me today."

"Duane."

"Duane," he said. "Said you took care of a problem for him and he appreciated it. Said he appreciated your respect. Speaking of diamonds, was you in our line of work you mighta earned one."

"I'm respectful as heck," I said. "But it wasn't me. It was some other handsome and intrepid investigator with a stentorian voice and razor-sharp wit."

"Whatever. Sound like just this once you managed to do something good by the Kings," he said.

I wondered if I should tell Marcus I was on my way to

the office to ring Social Service and the police in Virginia Beach and alert them to the nefarious schemes and addresses being employed by ne'er-do-wells in Duane's territory.

Probably not. I should let him enjoy the afterglow of me not being a pain in the neck. This one time.

10

The following morning I punched up Twitter on my computer, just like the cool kids did.

Grady Huff had ten followers on the social networking site. All ten were white supremacy groups. Most of his tweets called for Barak Obama and Joe Biden and Hillary to be jailed or worse. He thought Hillary deserved a good raping. That'd show her.

He only had ten followers but he followed three hundred. I scanned the list—many of them appeared to be former schoolmates at Episcopal High School. None followed him back; a bad sign in the Twitterverse.

Guys like me, we got friends for life, he had told me.

I checked his Facebook profile. Same story—lots of hate and no friends, no family.

He mentioned getting Candice off the internet. Not a recommendation from a friend or family member. Like he performed a Google search instead of calling his powerful friends for advice.

So far, what did I know?

An obese man in jail with no friends kept calling me

fatty, worried acquaintances from his old high school might find out he had feelings for the cleaning lady, the one he'd shot without remorse.

I called Candice Hamilton. She answered on the first ring.

I said, "Grady and Juanita were romantic."

"That's my guess too. It's impossible to prove, though," she said. "He won't admit it. There's nothing on either cellphone. No signs of recent intercourse, coerced or otherwise. No flowers, no love notes, nothing."

"Did the Franklin County police do an investigation?"

"Not much. Grady confessed. Why waste resources, you know? We're fighting an uphill battle."

I asked, "When did he buy the gun?"

"Three days before he shot her."

"Can you inform a jury that purchase was an unfortunate coincidence?"

"Sure, if I want them to think I'm a liar."

"We cannot give up," I said.

"That's the spirit."

"We cannot let Darren Robbins win."

"What is it with you and that guy?" she asked.

"It's complicated. I don't even know what he looks like, actually."

"He's quite handsome."

I hung up on her. She and Grady Huff, both delusional.

JUANITA YATES HAD a public Facebook profile. She was a cutie, indeed. Open and innocent face, at least ten years younger than Grady Huff. Only a few photos, very few friends. Most photos were of her smiling by herself. One in a yellow bikini that I'd bet money Grady gazed at for hours.

Her final post confessed that she would be falling asleep that night thinking about a special someone. One person had liked it—Grady Huff.

Be nice if I could figure out a way to check their Facebook messages. A weird thought, trying to trap the defendant into admitting he loved the victim, which was the easiest way to reduce his sentence. Hah, gotcha, now you only go to jail for ten years instead of forty, sucker.

A beautiful lonely girl. A rich ugly lonely guy. Romance. Then homicide.

But how did I prove it? And why would he kill her? Was it an accident? Was she breaking up with him? Was I wrong about the romance? She refused him and he was jealous? Or maybe he was refusing her? Or maybe Grady was just an irredeemable ass.

I drove to Grady's house off Lakewood, not far from Westlake. Took forty minutes. The air felt damp and loose. His was one of two houses for sale in the secluded neighborhood. Grady's was a modern double A-frame with a truly spectacular view of the lake. The poplar was already turning a bright yellow and soon the neighborhood would be brilliant with fall. The booklet attached to the For Sale sign listed the price at just under nine hundred thousand.

A lawn crew was mowing the neighbor's lot, getting in a final shave and payday before the weather grew too cold for growth. I waited by their truck until one of the workers, a good ol' hardworking Franklin County boy wearing a bright orange vest and camo hat, stopped his machine nearby.

"Help you, sir?" he asked.

Ah manners. Manners maketh the mower.

I held up a twenty dollar bill and slipped it under the

wiper blade of the truck. "I'd like to buy you lunch, if that's okay."

"What for?"

"Anything you can tell me about Grady Huff. I'm working on the case."

"Guy who killed Juanita," he said.

"That's the one."

"Yeah we mowed his yard. Still do, but the real estate guy pays now. Total jackass. Grady, I mean, not the real estate guy."

"I've met Grady. And I concur, he's full of jackassery. Any idea why he did it?"

"Got no idea, sir." He went to his truck for fuel and began dumping it into the mower's tank. "The cleaning lady, though, Juanita? She was here a lot more often than for just cleaning the place, if you follow me."

"You believe there was romance afoot."

"Yeah or something."

"Did you know Juanita?" I asked.

"Spoke with her on occasion. She doesn't know much English. *Didn't*, I mean, scuse me, sir. But she seemed right pleasant. Real pretty too. Dunno why she's boppin' bottoms with someone like Grady Huff."

"That is precisely what I'm endeavoring to discover."

"Wish I knew. I'd tell ya, sir."

"What car did she drive?" I asked.

"Don't remember. An old beater of some kind."

"How'd she dress?"

"Don't remember. Comfortably, I suppose."

"She ever come with anyone? Say anything odd?"

"Not that I recall," he said. "But I only met her a handful of times. Like I said, sweet lady."

I slipped my card under the wiper blade too.

"You remember anything else, call me."

"Yes sir, be happy to." He started the mower again. "Being honest, I hope the bastard fries!" he shouted and roared off.

I went around the house to check all the doors and accessible windows. Everything was locked. I moseyed to the deckhouse and boat. Both had been cleaned and sanitized, nothing useful remained.

I called the real estate number and left a message.

This part of the county had only a small police substation, which meant the homicide investigation had been handled by the sheriff's department. I drove to Rocky Mount and parked downtown. The Whole Bean Coffeehouse intercepted me en route, insisted I buy a cup of coffee and demanded it be eaten with a scone. With no other options, I acquiesced. The downtown held old world charm, character and integrity dating back to the fifties and sixties, and I enjoyed the sights while finishing off the tyrannical dessert.

The sheriff himself invited me back to his office and we sat on opposite sides of his desk, which also held the charm and integrity of the sixties. The desk was wood and so was his chair. Everything was wooden, including the paneling and the picture frames.

In a stupefying and wonderful display of serendipity, two basketball books were on the shelf, both written by Wooden. John Wooden. Everything was wooden.

It's the little things in life that bring me joy.

I said, "Makes it easy, doesn't it, when the guy confesses."

Sheriff Sutton was steely-eyed, steely-haired, and soft spoken. His uniform was ironed crisply. Each button in place. He steepled his fingers, elbows on the wooden armrests. "You know, Inspector, I think Mr. Huff truly believes he's above the law. Like this will pass him by because of his net worth. Why not admit it if you won't be held accountable, in his eyes."

I liked that he called me Inspector.

"Was there a simulacrum of an investigation?"

He did not shrug. Did not shake his head. Made no discernible gestures. "Only what was necessary. All evidence indicates Mr. Huff shot Ms. Yates with the handgun we found on the dock, and his story corroborates. Be nice to know why, but he offered no explanation."

"He has no family or friends, from what I can tell."

"Correct," he said, like a statue would say correct. "Both parents are dead, no siblings. He didn't call anyone while in our custody."

"Does Juanita Yates have a next of kin?"

"We're still working on that. So far we've been unable to discover...well, anything. Not even her address. We conclude she was here illegally and that Juanita Yates was not her real name. Apparently a woman stopped by to collect her things several months ago, on my day off. We wouldn't release anything to her and so she left. I don't have a photo of the woman."

I wished he would call me Inspector again.

I asked, "What things did Juanita have for the woman to collect?"

"Nothing, essentially. We wouldn't release the cellphone or car, and those are the only two things with any value. Juanita Yates wore no jewelry and had nothing significant in her handbag."

"Who is the car registered to?"

"Guy lives up near Radford. Claims the car was stolen from his driveway months ago but never reported it," said the sheriff.

"Did you investigate further?"

"No. Like I said, we got a confession and the culprit behind bars."

"Did you ever wonder if Juanita was a prostitute?"

"Sure. But the neighbors had seen her hauling in cleaning equipment, even when he wasn't home. And the house was obviously cleaned on a regular basis."

"Hmmmmm," I said intelligently.

"You're part of the defense team. Surely Mr. Huff doesn't have a chance."

"You only say that because I'm not flexing. Our goal is to get the charges dropped from first degree murder to something less than what he deserves. Either way, he'll be much older the next time he's a free man."

"I know the feeling."

"Come now, Sheriff Sutton. Look at this office with all its wooden glory. What more could a man ask?"

He said, "You were an officer?"

"I was, for about ten years."

"I was still a baby at ten. Talk to me again in twenty years."

"Mind if I examine the evidence you have in the locker?" I asked.

"My assistant can fax a waiver to Mr. Huff's attorney, and once we've received it then you're welcome to examine the evidence. There isn't much."

"I'm like Emmitt Smith. I can make a lot out of nothing," I said, pink with optimism.

Twenty minutes later I begrudgingly admitted the sheriff was correct. There wasn't much.

Grady Huff was gonna swing.

11

That evening Kix sat in his pen working out the grand mysteries of life by cracking plastic blocks together. In an hour, the Nationals would begin game five of a playoff series they were destined to lose. I had chili simmering on the stove and a cocktail chilling over ice in my Yeti. No one else had come home yet.

My phone buzzed. A text from Ronnie.

>> **Hello handsome stranger.**

>> **My pseudo-fiancé, Darren Robbins, is in town.**

>> **I'm going out with him this evening.**

I replied, **I hear he's attractive. Also I hate him.**

>> **I'm wearing minimal makeup and a turtleneck.**

>> **We're going to a public place. A restaurant.**

>> **And I'm dumping him.**

>> **To-Night. I will not wait one minute more.**

I was texting near the foot of the stairs and I felt the earth shift under my feet. Chili forgotten on the stove, I sat down on the bottom step and watched my phone suspiciously. Was it playing a joke on me?

I texted, **Want a getaway driver?**

>> No. Thank you.
>> I'll be fine.
>> Wish me luck.
I'll do even better.
I'll beseech the Almighty on your behalf.
>> Does that work if I'm not a believer?
Maybe that's part of His master plan.
Answering prayers to win us over.
>> No one's THAT nice.
>> Maybe I can come over afterwards?
>> We could...talk? And hold hands?
>> And pretend none of my past happened?
>> And pretend we're a happy couple?
>> And do some things that couples do?
If you insist.
>> Yes Mackenzie. I insist.

I replaced my phone and stood. Paced the kitchen twice. Took a sip of my drink, a Dark and Stormy. Paced the kitchen again. Drained the cocktail. Drummed my fingers on the counter. Eyeballed the pot of chili and went to the fridge for more peppers and ground beef.

Kix looked at me inquiringly.

"When in doubt," I told him. "Make extra. Just in case."

He rolled his eyes.

TIMOTHY AUGUST and I ate chili together on the couch and watched baseball until he went upstairs to read around 8:30. Kix nearly brought the house down at bedtime, shaking the walls for twenty minutes. Manny texted he wouldn't be home.

I cleaned dishes and watched the final innings. The

Nationals, obviously, lost. The season ended as it always did —too soon and with promise unfulfilled.

I got a third Dark and Stormy and watched the late game. And didn't look at the clock. And didn't worry about Ronnie. And didn't get up and pace every five minutes.

By eleven I could no longer stand it.

I messaged her, **Text me.**

Let me know you're alive.

And that you're not trapped under something heavy.

She didn't reply immediately.

I sat on the couch and rooted against the Dodgers and tried to breathe normally.

Finally, after a century had passed...

>> **I'm alive.**

>> **Thank you for checking.**

>> **Will text you tomorrow.**

>> **Goodnight.**

I stared long and good at the phone, willing another message to appear.

None did.

Good thing I wasn't attached to her. Good thing I was giving her space to solve her own problems. Good thing I was in total control of myself and my emotions and never got jealous and never succumbed to irrationality. Good thing I wouldn't worry about her all night.

Mackenzie August and Grady Huff, two guys not delusional at all.

12

Sheriff Stackhouse called the following morning as Kix and I glared at each other over a spoonful of apple sauce.

"Hey babe. Got a second?" she said through the speakerphone.

"I've got so many seconds. I've got the greatest seconds."

Kix scoffed.

Stackhouse said, "I promised not to tell but you're going to catch wind sooner or later. Just don't blab you heard it from me. Kay?"

"Tell me."

"A guy named Darren Robbins beat the hell out of Ronnie last night."

I stood, knocking over my chair. "Details?"

"According to witnesses, he dragged her out of Martin's by her hair around ten. He had two goons with him. Police were called but no one saw what happened. She won't press charges. Her story is she got mugged. But her face is a mess and she's got broken ribs. She went to urgent care instead of the ER so we couldn't find her. Took me a couple hours but I found her anyway."

"How is she?"

"Mad. Brave. Scared. Still beautiful, somehow."

I said, "Where the hell was Fat Susie?"

"You know someone named Fat Susie? Is he the heavy man who was at your house recently?"

"Never mind. Thanks for the tip." I hung up.

I DROPPED Kix off at Roxanne's a few minutes early and then swung by Ronnie's apartment building. Her car wasn't there.

She was at her office, her red Mercedes in the usual spot.

Her receptionist hadn't arrived yet, or perhaps had been given the day off. Ronnie sat at her desk, a bag of ice pressed against her face. Both eyes had purpled and her lip was busted. Every inch of surface area looked swollen.

I blinked away tears.

Ronnie watched me as I stood in the doorway.

She said, "Come in and sit, Mackenzie. Before you go kill someone."

I obeyed.

She alternated the cold pack between her lip and her left eye. With her free hand she took a small sip from a glass —ice and gin, probably. An open bottle of ibuprofen sat near her keyboard. She said, "You're trembling."

"I'm processing emotion. A lot of them."

"Is one of them anger?"

"Yes."

"At me?" she asked.

"Of course not."

She released a breath of air. Like she'd been holding it. "I'm relieved."

"You could take the day off, you know."

"In theory. But what would I do? Sit alone, bored and afraid? Instead I'll do half-assed work and sip gin," she said. "And pretend my face doesn't hurt."

"Somehow," I said. "You're even prettier."

"I was hoping to avoid you a few days."

"Why."

She pointed at her face with her free hand.

"You told me a year ago that you liked me just because. I've thought about it ever since. But no one could love this face. And my face is all I have," she said.

"That's not true. Your gluteus is also divine."

"I did it. I broke up with Darren. I told him we're through. I told him I would no longer visit him or his clients. He wouldn't take no for an answer but I said it anyway."

"Your spirit," I said. "And your bravery. Are also divine."

"Mackenzie."

"Yes Ronnie."

"You cannot go kill him."

"The hell I can't," I said.

"I don't need your help. Nor do I want it. You can't undo the violence."

"I can prevent it from happening again."

"You're smarter than this, Mackenzie," she said. "Only neanderthals think that they can prevent future violence by answering past violence with more violence."

"I cannot and will not do nothing."

She pointed at her face again and leaned forward. "I earned this. One of the reasons I fell for you, you never talk down to me. You never belittle women. You never imply you're smarter or stronger, even when you are. I earned this. Don't try and take it from me."

"You earned it," I repeated.

"Yes."

"You're proud of the damage."

"Of course. You taught me to be."

We sat in silence, listening to cars on Salem Avenue coming off Gainsboro and Williamson. I struggled through her logic. She patiently gave me time for it.

A woman's heart is a deep ocean...

She pressed her hand against her ribs and shifted, trying to get comfortable. My ribs had been broken several times and it was no use. No comfort could be found.

I said, "You're proud. Because you were scared but you stood up to him, you survived his rage, you took his punishment, and you didn't give in. And afterwards you got the injuries treated without notifying the police. And you did it independently."

"Yes."

"You wanted to stand up to him for months or years and you finally did it. And it took every ounce of courage you had. And if I go beat him up I will be sending the message to Darren that you needed help. And I will be sending the message to you that I don't think you're strong enough to handle it."

She nodded, switching the ice bag to her other hand and wiping the moisture from her palm onto her pant leg. "You're giving words to emotions I haven't fully thought through, but yes. Also I threatened to expose him, so if you interfere he'll think I was bluffing."

"Expose him how?"

"By producing evidence of our illegal business arrangement."

"Are you bluffing?" I asked.

"I'm not. I have proof. It would ruin me too but the threat is one of the few cards I'm holding."

"What if he had killed you?"

"Then I would have died being brave. I would have finally paid for my sins. And you would have my permission to kill him."

"Where was Fat Susie?"

"I lied to Reginald. I told him I was staying in. Please do not be mad at him, Mackenzie. Besides there were three of them, what could Reginald do?" she asked.

I nearly pulled the armrest off her client chair at the thought of three of them.

"This is requiring a lot from me," I said.

"I know."

"I'm fighting every impulse I have."

"I know that too. But I'm worth it." She smiled. The tug at her busted lip made her wince. "Darren can't kill me. Not yet. I'm too important to his plans."

"I cannot and will not do nothing. But for you, I will wait. Until I find an excuse. A reason to kill him that has nothing to do with you," I said.

"I know you're a violent man. No, perhaps that's not the correct terminology. I know that you're capable of violence and destruction. More so than anyone I know. But could you really kill him? And not think twice?"

"Like stepping on a roach."

"That's a little...spooky," she said.

"And arousing?"

"Everything about you is arousing. Except maybe that."

"So," I said. "Does this mean you're single?"

She started to smile but it hurt. So she pressed her lips together and instead let the chroma of her blue eyes intensify. "I am single."

My heart, the feeble coward, did a somersault.

"Want to go out? On a date? With me?"

"Yes, more than anything. But not until my face heals," she said.

"I can cook you dinner at my place or yours. Wounds look good on you."

"Ask me again in a week. I need this to heal for more reasons than mere vanity. I need fully functional mouth muscles during our first date," she said.

My heart, the unforgivably weak milksop, nearly stopped. I felt a little lightheaded.

"I do not kiss on the first date," I said.

"Yes you will. For hours, you will."

Her law firm's front door opened. A moment later, Fat Susie came into her inner office with two coffees and some doughnuts.

He froze. Looked at her face. Looked at me.

"Oh shit," said Fat Susie.

"Yeah," I said.

"What happened? Oh shit, man."

"Nothing happened which you could have stopped, Reginald," said Ronnie.

He kept his eyes on me. "You gonna kill me, man?"

"No he's not. Mackenzie was just leaving."

"I am?" I asked.

"Please."

I stood. Gave her a final look. Then glared at Fat Susie.

"Reginald," I said.

"Yessir."

"Where she goes, you go."

"Yessir."

"She goes to the bathroom, you go too," I said.

Ronnie balled up scrap paper and threw it at me. "Out," she said.

13

Franklin County's sheriff didn't care much about Grady Huff's victim, Juanita Yates. The sheriff wasn't being crass or heartless—he was being efficient. He'd made an attempt to find her next of kin, but they were hiding so he didn't pursue it further. Probably they were here illegally, which would put him in a tough spot.

Ergo the sheriff didn't know her identity.

And Grady Huff didn't want me to discover it.

Which meant that's what I was gonna do.

I spent the day bothering Grady Huff's neighbors and learning nothing. Everyone agreed it was sad and horrible what happened to the cleaning lady but no one knew a thing about her, not even a name until they saw it on the news. She didn't clean their houses. In fact, I found no evidence that she cleaned any house other than Grady's.

Ah hah. A clue!

And yet I still knew nothing.

Her cleaning supplies were purchased from Walmart, which was a dead end. According to the Franklin County sheriff, Grady told the homicide guys that Juanita had answered a Craigslist ad he posted, looking for a house cleaner. He'd fired the last two services, which weren't good enough for royalty like him.

I got lucky leaving the lake. I stopped by the Spirit station for gas, the one near Homestead Creamery. Went inside for health food like chips and a candy bar. The store was empty, other than me and the guy working the register.

He was Hispanic. On a whim, I showed him Juanita's photo from Facebook.

"Do you know this girl?" I said.

"Sorry mister," replied the guy. A young kid, early twenties. "Juanita is dead."

Eureka. I might splurge and get TWO candy bars.

"How'd you know her name?"

"Always she come here for gas," he said.

"What do you know about Juanita?"

"Nothing. She spoke Spanish but we did not talk much," he said.

"How often was she in here?"

"Two days a week, always."

"Always?"

"Yes sir."

"That's a lot of gas."

"Yes sir," he said and nodded politely.

"How much did she get?"

"I do not understand."

"Did she fill up her tank?"

"Yes sir," he said. "Over ten gallons. Always two days a week."

"Was Juanita nice? Kind? Mean? Aloof?"

"She was...normal. One time we told our names, but I don't know any thing."

"What time of day?" I asked.

"I do not remember."

"Which direction was she heading?"

"I do not remember. That way, I think." He pointed towards the lake, towards Grady Huff's house.

"Did she ever have friends with her?"

"No sir. She was alone."

"What kind of car?"

"I do not remember. Blue, maybe. Or white."

"Does anyone else know her?"

"I don't think."

"Twice a week," I said.

"Yes sir."

"Which days?"

"I do not remember. Maybe the beginning and the end. Monday and Friday. Maybe," he said.

I slid him my card and three candy bars and a fifty.

"You remember anything, you call me. And this delicious Snickers is for you. And keep the change."

He nodded again, clearly overcome by my magnanimity.

I MET Candice Hamilton for drinks at Stellina, a quiet bar in downtown Roanoke. She rubbed her eyes, fatigued from staring at documents the past ten hours, and quickly drank an amaretto sour. Then ordered another to nurse.

Stellina was small and darkish, most of the light tinged red from colored lamp shades. We sat at the bar and talked and pondered the splendor of liquor bottles across the polished wooden counter.

Candice Hamilton was attractive. Enough so that most of the guys checked her out. The day had been warm and she wore a skirt, and her legs got second glances. She was fit and thin and her hair was shiny and soft, a girl-next-door appeal.

She said, "You seem to think her frequent stops for gas are indicative of something."

"Juanita didn't clean the other houses nearby, so she was coming here just for Grady. And based on gas consumption, coming from a ways off. I bet she didn't live in Franklin County."

"So we might never find her," said Candice and she checked her phone.

"Do not be faint of heart. I'm more intelligent than I appear."

"I wish I had your confidence. I'm filing motions as fast as I can and getting nowhere."

"Would it help if Darren Robbins was dead?" I asked.

She smiled and it brought out her laugh lines. I was charmed. She said, "Probably not, though be my guest."

"I've been told I can't, not without good reason."

"Who told you?"

"Someone wiser than I," I said.

"Sounds that way. Is this someone a lady friend?"

"She is. One of my favorites. Though we remain platonic."

She swirled her drink and checked her phone. "Her choice?"

"Mine. But...perhaps not for much longer."

"Sounds complicated. Isn't it always the case," said Candice, watching me.

"It's fishy," I said, bringing us back to a topic over which I wasn't afraid to make eye contact. "Juanita Yates is fishy. A stolen car? No other customers? No logical motive in her death? I'm terribly perplexed."

"Police can't find anything about her. But you can?"

"I'm hot on her trail. For Grady Huff I would move mountains," I said.

She raised her glass. "To Grady Huff."

I clinked hers with my Old Fashioned. "To Grady."

"And his deep pockets. May he rot in prison."

Her phone vibrated. She opened and grinned at a few incoming bright photographs. She held the screen so I could see—pictures of a toddler, a little girl.

"My baby," she said. "Tyler."

"Tyler's a boy name."

"My Tyler is a girl. Don't be base."

"Where is Tyler?" I asked.

"At home in Sterling. My mother's watching her, and she sends me photos and videos. I cry five times a day, missing her."

True to her word, she leaked tears from both eyes.

"Tyler's father?" I asked.

"There is no father."

"Immaculate conception," I said wisely. "Way to go."

"Anonymous donor from a clinic. Until this trial is over I don't even have time to visit on the weekends, and it's killing me."

"Bring Tyler here to Roanoke."

She wiped her eyes. "It wouldn't work. A hotel room is no place to keep a toddler the entire day. Up there, my mother has daycare help."

"Tyler is welcome at my son's daycare. A lovely lady named Roxanne keeps him at her house," she said.

"You have a son?"

"His name is Kix. He's not walking yet. And shut up about it," I said. "One day he'll walk and he'll be the best walker and it'll be glorious."

Candice smiled wider and wider. Those had to be porcelain veneers. "His name is Kicks? Like, the soccer player kicks the ball? And you're making fun of Tyler?"

I glared appropriately. "Kix, as in he kicks Tyler's butt."

"Could Tyler really stay with Roxanne? It's baby proofed? Is Roxanne trustworthy? You vetted her? Does she have a teaching degree? You checked her background?"

"Polygraph every other week," I said. "Direct descendant of Abraham Lincoln. She's ordained, a Nobel prize winner in childcare, fluent in sign language and Latin. And her PBJ sandwiches are on point."

"You're mocking me. But Tyler is all I have," said Candice and she cried again.

"Then bring her. I'll call Roxanne to verify."

"Mack," she said and she sniffed. "That would be beyond tremendous."

She stood and wiped her eyes and hugged me. One of those hugs where she leans in hard, and her face presses against my throat, and both arms go around my neck and squeeze. It was a good one.

Mackenzie August, Mr. Beyond Tremendous.

14

Manny used his clout as a federal marshal to get the Franklin County sheriff to release the stolen car used by Juanita Yates. It wasn't being used in the homicide investigation anyway. Hell, there wasn't an investigation period.

The car was a blue Jeep Cherokee, twenty years old, 156k on the odometer. I drove it up Route 8 through Floyd from Rocky Mount; the trip took ninety minutes on back country roads. Manny followed in my Honda.

The Cherokee had been stolen from a man named Brent Lowe a year ago, or so he claimed. Brent lived near Claytor Lake, a popular spot for tourists and vacation homes in the mountains. Brent didn't live on the luxurious side of the lake, though—he lived on Trade Winds Road in a trailer near a handful of others.

I parked at his trailer and climbed out. The air up here felt thin and cold. The leaves had already begun turning.

Manny parked on the street and got out. He leaned over and groaned. "Those country roads, amigo. Gonna be sick."

"Don't throw up on my spaceship."

"Ay dios mio, gonna die," he said.

The grass was long and brown in this neighborhood. I climbed the wooden stairs to Brent Lowe's door and knocked. It sounded hollow and flimsy.

A man answered. He wore sweatpants and a Jimmy Buffet style flower shirt and thick socks. Open and friendly face, short gray hair. He held a glass of...something in his left hand. Maybe coffee mixed with milk, a dirty white concoction.

"I'll be dammed," he said. He grinned and it looked like he enjoyed doing it. "There she is, Old Blue."

"Brent Lowe?" I asked.

"That's me. And that's my car. Never thought I'd see her again."

"Courtesy delivery from Sheriff Sutton."

He stuck out his thick hand and we shook. "Mighty obliged to you. Thought the sheriff said the car was evidence or some such."

"Not anymore," I said.

"Say, is your friend sick? Does he need some Maalox or something?"

Manny had sat down on the gravel, his head between his knees.

I said, "What he needs is an iron constitution, the pansy."

"Why is Old Blue no longer evidence?" asked Brent Lowe. He meandered across the deck in his socks, down the stairs, and towards the Cherokee. His neck needed shaving, covered in heavy fuzz.

"Are you familiar with the case for which your car was impounded?" I asked. And then I observed him intensely, the way Inspector Clouseau would.

In my professional opinion, he looked sad.

He said, "Yeah I heard about it. Girl who stole the car got shot."

"Right. Her name was Juanda."

"Juanita," said Brent Lowe. He corrected me without thinking.

Ah hah!

I was so preternaturally talented at my job, I scared myself.

"Right, Juanita."

"Yeah that's a real shame," he said.

"You knew Juanita?"

"Knew her?" He shook himself, taking his eyes off the Cherokee. "No sir, I didn't know her. But I guess she's the one who stole my car, huh?"

"Why'd you never report the theft? You seem attached to the car," I said.

"Oh well. Old Blue ain't worth much anymore, I reckon. Juanita needed it more than me. I got a bike round back in the shed, I can drive."

"But you kept paying insurance on Old Blue, all this time," I said.

"Did I? How about that. Stupid of me, huh."

"Anyways, that's no business of mine," I said. I grinned—ah shucks, I's being too nosey for my own good. "Here's your car. Key's in the ignition. We'll be on our way."

"Thanks again!" said Brent Lowe with a lot of genuine enthusiasm. "Tell the sheriff I appreciate it."

I got into the Honda's passenger seat. Manny reluctantly slid behind the wheel.

I asked, "Do you think it's a coincidence that Juanita was cleaning houses at Smith Mountain Lake, and the car she drove had been stolen from Claytor Lake?"

"Don't talk," he said. "I a nauseated spic."

"Know what those two lakes have in common?"

"Water. Don't be stupid."

"Money," I said. "People with money to burn."

"I don't care. What now?" he asked. "Ride a roller coaster? Spin in a circle till we throw up?"

"I had planned on observing Brent and Old Blue, unbeknownst to them, from a magnificent hiding spot. However," I said. This was a sleepy street with no trees, no traffic, and no hiding spots. I'd be seen anywhere. "I think we'll go with our backup plan."

"*Simon*," he said, which meant 'Yup' in Spanish. Or so he claimed. "Let's find the straightest road leading to Roanoke."

I turned on my phone and opened the location services app.

On the screen, I was represented by a blue dot.

Brent's Cherokee was represented by a orange dot—the tracking device hidden in the truck, putting off a clear cell signal for the next seventy-two hours.

My backup plan; I'd track Old Blue.

"I'm so good at this, it's scary," I said.

Manny groaned. "I'm going to be sick."

15

That afternoon at three I called it quits, giving me time to make football practice. Our final game was soon, which was good because my absences had grown embarrassingly frequent. I shrugged into my soft shell jacket and locked up. Temperatures had fallen into the fifties and a cold breeze came down Campbell Avenue.

I turned the corner onto 1st Street and nearly collided with Darren Robbins.

The Darren Robbins.

Darren wasn't as tall as me but it was close. He had short blond hair, styled with gel. Clean face, hard jawline. Eyes so brown they appeared black. Looked like he played quarterback in college and kept the muscle. Handsome and all-American, the kind of guy you want your daughter to bring home.

So you could punch him in the nose.

He wore a dark suit and a camel overcoat.

"Mackenzie August," he said. His hands were gloved and they hung by his side, the fingers twitching a little.

Darren had a shadow. Guy with a shaved head, wearing

jeans and a sports coat. The coat covered the bulge of his shoulder rig, but the pistol was in his coat pocket, hidden and pointed at me.

"Hey, look'it this. It's the man himself, the guy who beat up Ronnie Summers," I said.

"Relax, August. Play it cool. You get to walk away from this, if you don't act like a freshman."

I said, "Good thing there were three of you the night you beat up Ronnie, otherwise your hands might've gotten tired from hitting her face. Three's better, that way you courageous gentlemen could take turns."

"Quite the mouth on you," said Darren Robbins, lowering his volume for the sake of our fellow pedestrians. "Especially for a man purported to be sexually active with my fiancé. Let's walk. Then we go separate ways."

I turned back towards the market, towards the crowds. He fell in step beside me, the shadow behind.

"You're wrong," I said.

"Concerning?"

I said, "Ronnie was engaged and I have scruples."

"So."

"I can spell scruples, if that helps."

He didn't respond.

I said, "There was no sexual activity. I know your engagement was a sham. But it still mattered to me."

"Was," he said. I heard a question behind the word.

"You got dumped."

"Only naive rookies believe everything they hear, August."

"I'm not sure what's worse, beating up your fiancée or beating up a girl who dumped you. I mean, neither are great."

"Veronica and I had an arrangement." His gloves hands

came together, his left hand playing with the ring finger on his right. "And she'll honor it."

"Or else?"

"Doesn't matter. She'll honor the arrangement. I'm giving her a few days to think it over."

"Good thing. She's a woman—little brain power, prone to flighty decisions. Am I right?" I said.

We reached Market Street and stopped on the corner, near Center in the Square. Roanoke denizens hurried to and fro, bundled against the chilly wind.

"What do you want, Robbins," I said.

"To enlighten you."

"Good. Always nice to glean enlightenment from a man who hits women."

"You see this." He indicated the commercial world around us. "All of this, the market, the restaurants, the law firms—that's one reality. The world most people see. The world where mothers take their children for ice cream and meter maids ticket cars and farmers sell fucking grapes. But gentlemen like Marcus Morgan and myself, we're a part of another reality. A world with its own rules and ways of doing things."

"The underworld," I said. "This is a fun story."

"Call it what you want. It's a violent place with enormous stakes. It subverts much of the surface world and underpins the rest. You've wandered into that world, Mr. August."

"Whoops."

"I'm trying to be patient. Out of respect," he said, "to Marcus. Because this is his territory. But you've wandered into my world, like an errant dog, now it's time you back away."

"An errant dog." I looked down at myself. "I knew I

should have worn my tighter shirt today. It's a slim fit, you know? You could see how strong and manly I am."

"You're on the junior varsity team, August. You don't fully get it, and I understand. But my tolerance for the antics is at an end," said Darren. "I need to return to Washington. So you—"

"You've given up on poor Grady Huff?"

"The Huff trial is merely an excuse to be down here. My real business is with Marcus and Veronica and you," he said and sniffed. "How'd you know about the Huff trial?"

"I'm working for the defense. Which means you don't stand a chance. I'm so good it's scary."

He paused and glared at me. As if one of us was an idiot.

"You're working with Candice Hamilton?"

"I am," I said.

"Why?"

"To piss you off."

"Why?"

"You gang up on women and abuse them. You prostitute them. You abuse your power and you blackmail. You have blonde hair but brown eyes, and that's a stupid combination. I could go on and on."

"What the hell is wrong with you, August?"

"For starters, scruples," I said. "Keep up."

"I don't care what happens to Grady Huff. He's part of the surface world I mentioned."

"Good. Because I'm getting his charges reduced."

"You couldn't possibly. The idiot confessed," said Darren.

"Run back home to Washington before you get embarrassed, is my advice. Grady will be dodging first degree."

"Grady's fate is sealed."

"Ah hah! What you don't know is—"

"Jesus," he said. "Shut up. I'm here for two reasons. The first, to guarantee the continued shipment of Calvin Summer's primary export. The second, to guarantee the continued shipment of Calvin Summer's secondary export, his daughter."

Hearing him describe Veronica as an export was like a physical shot to the gut. I fended off a bout of dizziness.

Mastering myself, I said, "And you're here to lose the Grady Huff case."

He did something like grinding his teeth. His shadow, the guy behind us with the gun, snickered. Cause I'm hilarious.

"I don't care about Huff. And he's getting first degree, all the way," said Darren.

"So you're going to lose the trial and you got dumped. That's a rough week. This special world you're in, it sounds sub-utopian."

He shook his head. Not looking at me. He was still tugging on his ring finger.

"Perhaps I'll remain in Roanoke a few extra days to kick your ass in court."

"We're not going to court. We'll settle on manslaughter or second degree before then," I said.

"You haven't passed the bar, August. You're repeating cute phrases learned late on a Tuesday night, watching a cop show on—"

"What did Ronnie say about continuing her services?"

I interrupted him and he didn't like it. He wore the expression of someone having an irritating conversation with a stupid detective on a stupid street corner.

He said, "As I explained, I'm giving her a few days to think it over. She's a smart girl. She'll—"

"For reasons which are too sophisticated for you to

comprehend, Ronnie asked me not to kill you," I said. Behind us, his shadow shifted, as if wondering if he should use the gun. "So I'm not. Yet. But I don't like you, Darren, and I'm looking for an excuse."

Darren stepped back and looked at his shadow and shrugged again. "This is like talking to a two-year-old. Why am I bothering?"

The shadow said nothing.

"The two reasons you're down here," I said.

"What about them?"

"First, the fields of marijuana. I don't care. I imagine Ronnie doesn't either. They should keep running smoothly for a while, is my guess. Second, Ronnie's services. That's up to her. From what I was told, she gave you her answer and didn't cave while you three asshats beat the hell out of her. So you've got responses to both questions. Now run home."

Darren said, "I think you're the reason she said No."

"Maybe partly. But also maybe she sees that you're not worth her time. That she's got a future without you in it. That she holds more power in the deal than you do, and that you can shove it up your ass."

He took a sudden step towards me. He kept his face calm. "Do you know what Veronica does when she visits me in Washington? I book three rooms at the Regis off K Street. And I line up her boyfriends in hour-long shifts. I work Veronica the entire night, running her between clients. I run her into rooms with senators and congressmen and MS-13 bosses and Camorra hitmen and billionaire junkies. Two nights in a row, sometimes three. By the end, she's sick and can barely move and I remind her that I'll throw her and her father in jail if she so much as sheds a tear. And then we repeat the process the following month. Don't talk to me about power. I wear her ass out."

I came very close to dying. Darren's shadow was behind me, gun in my ribs. I didn't care. I wanted to put an uppercut into Darren's teeth. A knee into his groin. An elbow into his throat. I went through my options, so angry that the emotion was a kind of color at the edges of my vision. I tasted the hate in the back of my throat.

I settled on an option.

To kill Darren and live.

Which meant waiting.

Which was so difficult it made me tremble.

If Ronnie could endure him, I could too.

Darren Robbins stepped back. He made a motion brushing his hands together, like dusting them off.

"Okay, August. I tried. You and Grady Huff, you're dead men."

He turned and walked towards 1st Street. His shadow walked backwards a few paces, gun pointed, and then he turned also.

16

I grilled hamburgers that night. My standards for burgers were high, as were any discriminating gentleman's, so I mixed the ground angus beforehand with blue cheese crumbles, spices, soy sauce, a little ranch, and an egg. I kept the grill hot so they came off with a crispy seared surface and pink interior.

I set six places at our table, not including Kix, and announced to my guests that dinner was served.

Timothy took two burgers and complimented them with lettuce, tomato, and a small smear of mustard.

Fat Susie got three, representing about a pound and a half of beef.

Both Manny and Ronnie Summers laid their burger onto a spinach salad, the prima donnas. Maybe that's why they were beautiful and I wasn't.

I crumbled some beef for Kix and had just sat down when Sheriff Stackhouse entered, the last invited guest.

"Okay," she said. "Squad car's parked out front in plain sight, like you asked. Mind telling me what the hell is going on?"

"Sure," I said. "Get food first."

Stackhouse kissed Timothy August on the head. She did the same thing to Ronnie, and then went for a burger and salad.

"Look at this kitchen," Stackhouse said. "You cook dinner for seven and it's spotless."

Ronnie's face was still bruised and she moved gingerly. She said, "I don't know how they do it. I wish I could rent a room at chez August. I'd be willing to pay upwards of three thousand a month."

"Don't overthink it, babe," said Stackhouse, settling at the table next to my father. She wore her work khakis. "Just seduce one of the owners and he'll let you stay for free."

I winced. "Not what a son wants to hear."

Timothy August took a bite of food.

A supremely smug bite.

Manny raised his fork and said, "I am willing to be seduced, Ms. Ronnie."

"Thank you, Manny," she said. "If Mackenzie turns me down once more, I will come knocking."

"Me and him, we share a bedroom, señorita," he said. "So it be awkward."

"Maybe for him."

Timothy winced. "Not what a father likes to hear."

Fat Susie looked like a man who wished he was at Applebees instead.

Stackhouse cracked a can of Sierra Nevada. "So, seriously, why do you want a squad car parked out front, kiddo? You got me spooked."

I set down my burger. Which was so perfectly cooked it might be considered a delicacy.

"Thank you all for coming. I will regale you with a story.

Some of it you know, some of it you don't, and none of it leaves the kitchen."

Kix said, *We'll see about that. I got a big mouth.*

"A bad man has come to town. Darren Robbins. He is a corrupt federal prosecutor who is on the take with the District Kings. He had connections with Ronnie's father, Calvin, and he's dismayed about Calvin's death. He is here to leverage and reinforce the local mafia concerning various matters of villainy, none of which is germane to our conversation. What matters is this—he is demanding the lovely and talented Ronnie marry him and move to Washington D.C. He won't take no for an answer, and he's threatening to kill her if she refuses. Today he visited me and told me to backoff. I responded as a petty adolescent would and so now I'm a marked man. My time runneth short."

Timothy had frozen, food half chewed. He covered his mouth and swallowed. He said, "Good lord, son. I thought you said you weren't involved with the local mob."

"They're very fond of me."

Ronnie asked, "What did you say to Darren?"

"I told him you could make up your own mind and that if he touched you again I was going to kill him."

Manny nodded approval.

"Were his goons with him?" she asked.

"One. Guy with a gun. Black. Shaved head."

"That's Dexter. Were you scared?"

"A little. But he can't shoot me in the middle of the market."

Stackhouse laid her hand onto Ronnie's. "Baby, press charges. I can bring him in and ruin him."

"I can't."

"Why not?"

I answered for Ronnie. "There is more to the story that

won't be shared. But let me assure you, if Ronnie presses charges then her life is forfeit. She has a way to exert pressure on Darren but only as a last resort."

"So you're not exaggerating about Darren's involvement with the Kings?" asked Stackhouse.

"I wasn't being hyperbolic. Darren works directly with some of the most powerful crime bosses in America. And right now he's fixated on Ronnie."

Fat Susie made an unhappy grunting sound. He'd already finished two burgers.

Timothy said, "Surely the police, the sheriff, and a federal marshal can do...something."

"That would go poorly," I said. "For everyone in this room. The Kings have judges and cops and lawyers in their pocket. Plus an army of thugs for hire. They're not above killing us all."

"Earlier today I was fretting about our library's software update," he grumbled. Although his tie was already loose, he tugged at it further. "Do you have a plan?"

Manny, who'd been eating unperturbed, said, "Big Mack always got a plan, señor."

Let's hear it, said Kix. *Because I am stressed.*

"The Kings don't want drama. They don't want to get tangled with Roanoke's sheriff and a federal marshal. It'd be bad for business. And Darren doesn't want to lose Ronnie. It's in everyone's best interest to be cool. So right now that's what we're doing. We're buying time to figure this out," I said.

"Except Darren told you that you're a dead man," said Ronnie. "And he doesn't joke about that."

"That only worries me because it endangers my family. Which is why I've asked Stackhouse to start leaving her car here. I doubt they'll make a move on this house and they won't go after my family outside of it. Again, that'd be bad for business. Darren has to be at least a little worried about repercussions. At some point they might decide a war is worth it, but that day is not today. The reward isn't worth the risk. Yet."

Manny said, "Why don't I just go shoot Darren in his ass? We be done with it."

"He's got help and they'll be ready for you. We need to try diplomacy first. Violence only as necessary," I said.

"Diplomacy?" asked Timothy.

"I'm going to arrange a meeting of the local nefarious power players. All should remain quiet until then. But to be safe, Stackhouse will stay here every night and park out front. Fat Susie will remain with Ronnie during the day and she will move into our guest bedroom in the evenings."

"If you insist," said Ronnie.

I avoided eye contact with her.

Stay focused, Mackenzie.

"Manny and I can be anywhere at a moment's notice," I said. "We'll regroup after the mafia meeting."

"Remember," said Ronnie. "If worse comes to worst, I have a way to humiliate and expose him. But at that point, any remaining shit would hit the fan."

"Maybe as a very last resort. I'd rather you not be embarrassed in the public eye."

"What about you?" Timothy asked me.

"Yes, I prefer you alive," she said.

"To be honest, I'm hoping one of them comes calling. It would reduce their numbers."

Timothy threw up his hands, a vexed motion. "Good grief, the hubris on you."

Stackhouse gave a little shrug. "It's kinda sexy."

The screen door at the front opened. Timothy jumped. Stackhouse turned in her seat to get a look.

Carlos walked in wearing his usual tight t-shirt. His shaved head gleamed under our small chandelier.

Manny and Fat Susie threw him a wave.

Timothy looked on in alarm.

"Carlos," I said. "Grab a hamburger. What brings you?"

"Manuel. He tells me about the trouble," said Carlos. He laid a bag on the couch and went for food. "I asked señor Marcus Morgan what to do and he say to stay with you. Unofficially."

"Could get rough, Carlos."

"You gave me back my life," he said. "It is the least I can do. My daughter and I, we are very happy."

Manny said, "Maybe Carlos, he can stay with Ronnie too."

"Probably," I said. "Her peril is the most mortal."

Ronnie placed her hand on my forearm. I remained calm. "Carlos should be with you. Darren's threat worries me."

"Don't let it. The hero never dies."

Ronnie pushed some blonde hair out of her face. "Manny, you'll help him stay alive?"

"*Simon*," he said. His salad was nearly gone. "Though Mack better at this than you know, I think."

"So we're all agreed?" I asked. "This is the plan?"

"Only in lieu of a better one," said Timothy, watching Carlos in his periphery. "This is a nightmare."

"Not for me," said Ronnie Summers. "It's like I have a family. And Mackenzie's finally invited me to sleep over."

Kix said, *Can the blonde sleep in my room?*

17

We drank cocktails until midnight, our motley crew squished onto the living room leather couches.

Then the intricate bedtime routines began.

I made everyone brush their teeth—Fat Susie in the main floor's half bath and Carlos in the kitchen sink. (They each bunked on a couch with a pillow and extra blankets.) Timothy August and Stackhouse used the master bath, of course. Leaving Ronnie, Manny, and me the other bathroom.

We all three fit, sharing the his-and-her sinks. Ronnie wore red pajamas, which Manny told her made her look like Santa's elf. She looked elegant and attractive doing everything, even brushing her teeth, despite the purpled eyes and puffy lips.

She finished and said, "Even your bathroom is neat and clean. How does a household full of men maintain this level of cleanliness?"

"We're fastidious and fragrant," I said.

"I dunno what he say, senorita, but we are neat and we use aftershave and deodorant and cologne. At least I do."

She said, "This sleepover is kinda fun."

"Sí, baby, the funnest."

"Do you believe all this is necessary?"

"Probably not," I said. "Depends on how angry the Kings are and how desperate Darren is. I don't think they'll attack us in our home, in a residential neighborhood. They'd prefer to play it cool and for this drama to blow over without incident."

"But it's wise for us to be safe instead of sorry."

"Right. If Darren gets lonely tonight and comes barging into your apartment, I'd rather you not be there," I said. "That's the real danger, one man's jealousy."

"Yours or his?"

"Good question," I said.

"I'm going to bed. It's been a long day," said Ronnie. She stopped at the bathroom doorway, one hand on the frame. "Although I wouldn't object to company for the next hour or three."

Neither Manny nor I spoke. Or moved. Or breathed.

My longing for her caused corporeal pain.

"Actually," she said. "Never mind. I just saw my reflection again. I'm not pretty enough yet. Good night."

She left. We heard the spare bedroom door close.

Manny said, "How long you two been dancing around like this?"

I said, "Fourteen months."

"And you two have not, ahh, *hacer el amor*?"

"We have not."

"Hell is wrong with you?"

"So many things," I said. "I lie awake at night wondering the same question."

"No, but let us be serious for *uno momento*. Educate an ignorant spaniard. What do you wait for?"

I turned on the cold water in the sink. Rinsed my tooth brush. Splashed some water onto my face and rubbed my eyes. Took a deep breath.

I said, "A bunch of stuff. She was engaged. She's trying to offload baggage and I'd make it worse. The timing never works. I'm trying to follow a path that recommends a high degree of purity. We both have too much pride, probably. You name it. We're a mess, amigo."

"Okay. *Bueno*, I see. But Ronnie Summers probably be the prettiest girl in the state. And somehow, she likes you."

"If we *hacer el amor,* it'd be over. I'd lose her."

"Why? How do you know?"

"It's anecdotal, but that's how it's always worked before. I'd rather not risk it."

"You white people," said Manny. "You overthink things. In Puerto Rico, we get married and yell at each other."

"Tempting," I said. "I'll give that option some thought."

NOISES IN THE HALLWAY.

According to my clock, it was three in the morning.

Manny sat up from his mattress on the floor, near the foot of my bed. His gun was already in his fist.

He listened and glared under the door at the light.

He said, "It's Ronnie. Girl footsteps."

I got out of bed and went into the hall.

Ronnie was in the bathroom. Sitting on the side of the bathtub, her head in her hands.

She looked up and smiled—a weary expression.

"Nightmare," she said.

"Have those often?"

"Usually during the day."

I rested my back against the wall and slid down until sitting on the floor, next to her. Our bare feet touched. Hers were prettier than mine.

"You probably have some PTSD," I said.

"Cute girls with law degrees shouldn't get that. We're supposed to float above the fray, trouble free."

I took her hand and squeezed.

"The most frustrating thing," she said, "is not that I'm bothered by memories of things I've been forced to do, but by memories of some evil part of me enjoying it."

"That's above my pay grade. But I'm positive that only means you're human."

She sighed and returned the pressure with her fingers. "Maybe I need something stronger than a holistic psychotherapist and spa days."

"Maybe in addition to. If anyone deserves spa days, it's you."

"Mackenzie."

I yawned. "Yes Ronnie."

"Thank you."

We stayed that way a long time.

18

The next morning we blearily consumed copious amounts of coffee. Timothy and Stackhouse went to work. Carlos and Fat Susie escorted Ronnie to her office, under strict orders Darren got nowhere near her. If he showed, they'd call me immediately.

With all the excitement it was easy to forget one pressing matter—Grady Huff was gonna swing.

I took Kix to Roxanne's.

Candice Hamilton was already there, inside meeting Roxanne and her daughter. She was dressed in black heels, a calf-length pencil skirt, and stylish white blouse, looking like a successful and trendy modern business woman.

Judging by Roxanne's embarrassed smile, she wished she'd worn something other than plaid pajama pants and a t-shirt that said 'Boss Mom.'

But I bet Candice would trade places with her some days.

Kix, Tyler, and Lucy hit it off at once, pointing, and shouting, and throwing toys with familial gusto. Sort of like grownups did, but we did it with class and alcohol.

Candice put Roxanne through a thorough cross-examination until I took her arm and pulled her out onto the sidewalk.

"Rest easy, counselor," I said. "The defendant is great and has kept my son alive for over a year."

"I know. It's just...shit, I know. I worry." Candice grabbed my hand with both of hers and we walked to our cars. That hand and arm still ached a little—I'd been shot in the forearm over the summer by Calvin Summers. "It'll be fine. Right? Tyler will be fine."

"Both Tyler and your mother will have good days today."

"You're right. Of course you're right. I just need to let go." Candice kissed my cheek suddenly. Then said, "Don't get the wrong idea. I'm not flirting with you. I'm just very grateful. And I wanted to kiss your face."

"I can't blame you," I said. "I've been working on this face for years."

"What are your plans?"

"I'm going to find Juanita Yates's family."

She asked, "What makes you confident you can locate them?"

"I'm so good it's scary."

"Do you want to get lunch?"

"If I get back in time," I said. "Then sure."

I HIT Interstate 81 and took it south towards Radford and Claytor Lake.

I rang Marcus Morgan en route.

He answered in his deep voice, "Morning, August."

"I hereby call for an assembly of the iniquitous and

sinister head honchos in Roanoke, which includes Darren Robbins."

"You want a meeting."

"Correct," I said.

"You hate meetings."

"At the moment, I believe diplomacy behooves all our best interests."

"Heard about your encounter with Darren," said Marcus. "And that now he's gotta put you in the ground."

"I am affright and atwitter with dismay."

"Believe it or not, August, I am a busy man. I run a big damn operation. Somehow despite you not being inside my enterprise, you use up a lot of my time and resources," he said.

"Is Darren your boss?"

"He is not. Although his word carries more influence with the powers that be. More credit."

I asked, "You're not a power that be?"

"Darren and I, we both be minority share holders. So to speak. Along with many other share holders. And at the present time? Darren holds more stock than I do. But we both more or less answer to the majority owners. You follow?"

"Yes. That was beautifully phrased."

"Good. I used small words," he said.

"What am I?"

"If we're Walmart, then you a shoplifter."

"That's...unkind. I think your metaphor fell apart," I said. "What's Duane? He the *capo dei capi*?"

"Most of us aren't Sicilian. Duane, he's a majority share holder. One of the lesser men sitting on the Board of Directors, so to speak."

"If little Duane is on the board, then I'm way more important than a shoplifter," I said.

"Maybe you the janitor that Walmart fired but he keep coming back," said Marcus.

"I'm hanging up. You arrange the meeting. Soon."

"Know what you are? You the weird guy at Walmart saying hello to everyone coming in," said Marcus.

"But Ronnie digs me."

"Maybe she get you promoted to delivery boy."

I HAD PLANTED a LandAirSea tracking device inside Brent Lowe's Cherokee, hidden under the carpet in the back. An app on my phone kept record of his location, and today I sat at Claytor Lake examining his movements on my map.

Yesterday evening, Brent drove Old Blue to a house on the north side of the lake and stayed for thirty minutes. According to Zillow, the house was a small brick ranch set by itself, a half mile from expensive lake-front homes on Cedar Point.

"Who'd you go see, Brent Lowe?" I wondered.

The cosmos responded with silence.

Grady Huff didn't have a lot of time before trial. And I had a hunch...

I dropped the Honda into drive and motored to the north part of the lake, to the small ranch Brent had visited. The driveway was gravel. An old Kia was parked out front and there was an adjacent dry spot, meaning another car had been here until recently, shielding the gravel from the morning's drizzle.

I zipped my black rain jacket against the chill and

knocked on the front door. Somewhere inside, a large dog barked.

A woman looked at me from the peekaboo window beside the door. Her voice sounded muffled.

"Yes? I don't need anything."

I stepped backwards off the porch, giving her space.

"Yes ma'am," I said. "I'm here on behalf of the Franklin County Sheriff."

You liar, said the cosmos.

"Okay," came the reply. She had what sounded like a Latin American accent. "I can listen."

"The sheriff doesn't want to cause you trouble," I said, making up lies as fast as I could. "He only wanted to update you on the Grady Huff case."

She didn't respond.

"The car driven by Juanita Yates has been returned to the owner. No more questions will be asked. Mr. Brent Lowe isn't in trouble and neither are you."

There was silence. And then came noises of the door being unlocked.

A woman stepped onto the porch, hugging herself. She was the spitting image of Juanita Yates, but twenty years older.

"The man? Grady Huff?" she asked.

"He's still in prison. And he's going to be there a long time."

She nodded to herself. "Good."

I was putting together puzzle pieces.

This was Juanita Yates's mother. Most likely friends with Brent Lowe. Or more than friends. Juanita had been using Brent's car, and they lied about it being stolen. They'd been afraid to talk with the sheriff for some reason, possibly due to her being here illegally.

Pure conjecture. But it was all possible.

"Yes ma'am," I said. "It is good."

"That's all?"

"Is there anyway I can help you? I know this has been hard."

"The sheriff…I didn't know…that he knew me," she said.

"Juanita was your daughter."

She paused. And looked down at her feet.

I said, "You'll never have to go to court or talk with anyone. I'm not here to create problems for you."

"Juanita was my daughter," she said.

"Yes ma'am. I know. I'm sorry."

She started to cry.

"It is a terrible feeling," she said. We were sitting on stools in her kitchen at the counter. The lights were out and rain had begun pattering on the windows. Her heat was turned off. A dog growled and scratched at the nearby bedroom door. "For your daughter to die. And the mother feel she cannot talk to the police."

"Why couldn't you?"

She made a noncommittal motion.

Freshly made tea steamed in two cups on the counter.

"The man, Grady Huff. He will go to jail," she said.

"His trial is soon. And yes."

"He will be in jail for life?"

"He'll be in jail for a long time. Exactly how long has yet to be determined," I said. My voice felt like it echoed in the house.

"A long time. Good."

"Do you know why Grady might have killed her?"

"Because he is a monster," she said. "Yes?"

Ms. Yates was pretty and she knew it. Despite being scared and bereft, she carried herself like a woman accustomed to men being drawn towards her. An expectation of preferential treatment. It wasn't arrogance; it was habit.

I got the feeling she used the accent and limited vocabulary to bludgeon lesser men into thinking her weak and lovable.

"I've met him. And I didn't like him," I said. "Was she living here with you?"

"No. She was alone. I was to come visit her home soon."

"Where?"

She made another noncommittal shrug. "I did not know yet."

"How many houses did she clean?" I asked.

"I do not know."

"Was cleaning her full-time job?"

"I do not know. She wanted..."

"Independence."

She put her hand on mine. "Yes. Thank you, Mr. August. She wanted independence."

"Were she and Grady Huff romantic?"

"No. She would not."

"How do you know?" I asked.

"She was a good girl. She was an angel."

"Had Juanita dated anyone else recently?"

"I don't know. No, maybe."

"Did you know she stole Brent Lowe's car?" I asked.

"I did not know."

"Do you know Brent Lowe?"

"I do not know him," she lied.

"How old was Juanita?"

"Twenty-four."

"Where did she go to school?" I asked.

"I teach her."

"Do you have other family?"

"No."

"None living at this house?"

She squeezed my hand. "No, Mr. August."

A second lie. I'd seen the evidence.

"How long have you lived here?"

She did another noncommittal shrug.

"Did you and Juanita send each other text messages?"

"No," she said.

"Did she ever mention Grady?"

"I don't know. No, maybe."

Around and around we went. Ms. Yates knew nothing. And when she did know something, it was always No.

After an hour of fruitless pestering, I walked to the door. She accompanied, still holding my hand and kind of leaning on me. She knew from experience—intimacy keeps the wheels greased.

"Thank you, Mr. August," she said.

I gave her my card. It had my name and number.

"Call me if you think of anything else," I said.

"I won't."

"I know."

"So Ms. Yates is hiding something?" asked Candice Hamilton. We were eating lunch at the Blue Apron restaurant in Salem. The table cloth was white and so were our napkins; between us sat a candle and fresh flowers. I had steak frites and a beer. Candice had a bibb lettuce salad with shrimp and something called a Red Rooster cocktail.

"She pretended she didn't know Brent Lowe, the owner of the stolen Jeep Cherokee. She pretended she didn't know the car was stolen, and she lied about not living with anyone but clearly she is."

"I can't believe you found her," said Candice. She reached across the table and speared a piece of my steak. "Do you mind? That looks amazing."

What in the hell.

I stayed cool. Barely.

Yes I did mind. More than words could convey.

I debated throwing the vase of pansies at her.

"Uh," I said. Focus, August. It's just steak. "The police weren't trying very hard."

"How does this help our case?"

"It might not. Maybe she's lying because she's here illegally and doesn't want to get mixed up in legal drama. Maybe her daughter Juanita truly was an angel."

"Wow, your steak is delicious," she said, eyeing my food.

Yes I KNOW.

I began shepherding the steak and frites closer to my side of the plate, away from the ravenous succubus.

"Or maybe," I said. "Ms. Yates is hiding something. Maybe not all is as it seems."

"Do you think?"

"I hope so. I don't know how to prove this was a crime of passion otherwise. They were romantic but Grady Huff won't admit it, because he's proud and because he's an idiot and an irredeemable ass. Maybe I can find another way to demonstrate their ardor."

"Speaking of ardor," said Candice. "Did you tick off Darren Robbins or what?"

"I plead the fifth."

"Suddenly today I'm getting all sorts of pushback from the Commonwealth's office."

"Like how," I said.

"I'm receiving redacted documents. Delays on discovery. They're being reticent with exculpatory evidence. And Darren is responding to my emails, where before it was the Commonwealth Attorney. They're forcing mountains of paperwork my way to eat up our time and clog the lanes. Up until today it was civil and collegial."

"Hm," I said intelligently. "I may have poked the bear too hard."

"Poked him how?"

"I ran into him downtown. Told him we were going to kick his ass."

She set her fork down. Made a groaning noise and rubbed at a spot between her eyebrows.

I sipped my beer the way a lesser and sheepish man would.

"Some sort of masculine pissing contest involving genitalia comparison?" she said.

"In retrospect, my imprecations were ill-timed. But I hate that guy."

"Told you he was handsome, didn't I?"

"Handsome like a donkey."

"Don't stress over it, Mackenzie. You're more attractive, in my opinion," she said, focusing hard on her cocktail.

"Goes without saying. But you should keep saying it anyway."

She smiled.

Mackenzie August, batting a thousand with the ladies today. Fat load of good it was doing me.

19

I spent the afternoon at football practice, helping as best an absentee defensive coordinator can. The head coach wanted strong role models around and I fit the bill, even if I didn't fully conform to his preferred schedule. Patrick Henry's first playoff game was tomorrow night and we were going to lose by a billion to a football powerhouse in northern Virginia.

Marcus Morgan observed practice, as was his wont several times a week, from the sidelines, arms crossed over his chest. He wore a steely expression and silver sunglasses and a black rain jacket. Afterwards he met me at the car and said, "Chilly."

"Maybe if you smiled more it would keep you warm."

"How's my boy?"

I pointed to the far side of the practice field to a couple guys chatting on the bleachers.

"Scouts from Liberty and JMU. Ask them."

"I don't want fucking Liberty and JMU," said Marcus.

"Jiminy Christmas, the mouth on you."

"I want UVA or William & Mary, a school known for something other than pretty white girls."

"Jeriah's only a junior. You still got time. But I happen to like pretty white girls," I said helpfully.

Marcus shifted in his jacket, like he was irritable. Made a tsk'ing noise.

"My son, Jeriah? Caught the jackass with blow in his room last night."

"Probably best I don't mention the irony."

"Probably," he said. "For the best."

"You know, because you're mad he had cocaine? And you yourself are this region's largest mover of cocaine."

"Yes, thank you, August. Good of you not to mention."

"That's what friends are for."

"I took his phone. He's been getting and sending nude photos," said Marcus.

"Of pretty white girls?"

"Of pretty white girls."

"Maybe Virginia Military Institute would be better."

He made a grunting noise, tinged with approval.

"The son of Marcus Morgan," he said. "Sent off to damn military school. But might be best."

"I'm sending Kix to the Naval Academy next year."

"Kix's two."

"No, he's still one," I said. "But he's advanced. Ready for the Navy, in my opinion. By the way, who's your new walk-around guy? Guy in the car, now that Fat Susie is with Ronnie?"

"That's Freddie. Mean guy. Don't like to talk. Fought MMA couple years. Changing subject—I made phone calls. All parties agree; we need to meet. Figure this shit out. Talk about Calvin's death, talk about marijuana, talk about Veronica Summers, talk about you."

"I bet you're tired of talking about me."

"I been tired of talking about you twelve long months, August."

I said, "Sometimes I think you say things intentionally to cause the maximum amount of hurt feelings."

"That's what friends do."

"When's the meeting?"

"Not long. Toby left town two days ago. Coming back tomorrow. Make this thing official."

The final football players were trudging off the field, grim and muddy.

"How's it work?" I asked. "You can't meet without a chaperone? Toby attended a few months ago too."

"We got rules. Commandments, a code. Organization. Otherwise we're a loose network of thugs. Me and Toby and Darren, the three of us make some decisions."

"Like during the summer, you and Toby decided I was justified in killing Antoine," I said.

"Right on. August, I gotta be honest. I don't see this one going well for you."

"Gasp."

"You a honky getting on everyone's nerves. And I wouldn't be surprised, Toby or Darren try to ace you sooner than that."

"Those sinister evil-doers," I said.

Marcus's stoic face, carved from granite, cracked.

"S'what I like about you. Professional hitman gonna come put a couple in your temple, you crack jokes."

"Yeah," I said. "I'm great."

THAT EVENING, Candice Hamilton arrived at Roxanne's at

the same time as me. We collected our children and stopped at the cars, Kix suspiciously eyeing Tyler.

Candice drove a small silver BMW. She looked relieved, patting her daughter's hair.

She said, "Tyler looks happy. Healthy."

"Maybe a little shrewish, though."

"Thank you for Roxanne. She's a life-saver."

"You're welcome," I said.

"What are you doing now?"

"Headed home. Think about dinner."

"Mind if I join?" she asked. "I want to put off paperwork as long as I can. That's all that waits for me at my hotel. I don't know anyone else and I'm sick of my paralegal."

"Sure," I said. "I live close."

"Just a few minutes. Maybe a drink."

"Sure," I said again.

I buckled Kix in and I got behind the wheel.

What a presumptuous harlot, said Kix.

"Candice is lonely."

And?

"And I'm kind."

She's a pretty harlot. Wearing heels. You love those.

"Doesn't hurt. And watch your mouth."

She takes it for granted she's invited over. And that you'll make her food and fix her drinks.

"Yeah. She does. But she's paying me a small fortune. Perhaps she's emboldened with some entitlement."

No good will come of this. Mark my words.

I drove to chez August and parked on the stone driveway. Manny was on the front porch, nailing white crown molding around the interior of the porch ceiling. He had designs on installing a fan so we could play chess and beat the summer humidity. He descended the step ladder and took Kix from me and talked Spanish to him, hell-bent on raising a bilingual boy.

Candice parked behind me. She emerged, holding Tyler. She stopped in the yard and gaped at Manny.

He had that effect.

"Might be a full house tonight," I told her. "This is Manny, my good friend. Manny, this is Candice."

"Hola! Dinner is salad. Needs tossing, but ready otherwise."

She nodded without sound and resumed walking, a little slower.

I opened the screen door for her.

"Thank you," she said.

She went inside, trailing Manny carefully, like beautiful people could go supernova any second. I started to follow but I noticed Ronnie's red Mercedes racing down Windsor.

My heart quickened with delight as it considered the sun goddess cargo within.

"Here comes the lady," I told myself. "Oh so light of foot."

She parked on the street and nimbly emerged. Fat Susie got out from the passenger seat. Carlos from the rear.

"It's like your car is trying hard to be culturally sensitive," I said.

She wore black and pink activewear, the expensive kind tailored to flatter and highlight a woman's body. It worked.

I didn't care what Fat Susie and Carlos wore.

"Hello Mackenzie. I have a plan," she said. Her face was less purple and more greenish-blueish now.

"Hello Ronnie. I'm listening."

She stopped walking when our toes touched. A wisp of

her blonde hair tickled my chin. I think she did that on purpose.

"I'm single, you know. You could kiss me. But don't," she said. "It would hurt. Would you like to hear my brilliant plan?"

"I would like to."

"Kiss me or hear my plan?"

"I would do anything," I said.

"If only that were true. Darren broke into my apartment last night and vandalized it."

I didn't say anything. But the muscles in my jaw and neck began clenching and bunching of their own volition.

She said, "He and Dexter, I think. Most of my stuff is ruined. Good thing I stayed at your place. In related news, I've decided to keep the marijuana fields to help replace my wardrobe."

"I should've killed him."

"It's just stuff. I'll get more. Anyway, here's my idea. I'm leaving town," she said.

"A stupid plan."

Fat Susie and Carlos went to the front porch like kids who didn't want to hear their parents whispering sweet nothings. They sat in rocking chairs.

She said, "There's a crisis going on in Virginia Beach. Police have rescued some girls from sex trafficking. Twenty or thirty girls. But they have nowhere to put them, so you know what those assholes did?"

"Put them in various jails for teenagers?"

"That's precisely what happened. And no one cares. Can you believe it? I'm taking my law degree on the road and I'm going to rattle their cages. I should be able to procure a better solution. And as an added bonus, I'll be out of town and out of danger, so you'll worry less."

"Maybe. However..."

"However what?" she asked.

"However, I'll be lonely."

"Good. You deserve to be. I could have been yours months ago. Maybe when I return my face will be healthy."

"I'd rather you not go alone."

"Would you like to accompany me?"

"I would," I said.

"But you cannot. I know." She looked over my shoulder. "Reginald, how much does Marcus pay you?"

From the front porch, Fat Susie said, "Mr. Morgan or anybody else, I get paid twelve hundred a week."

"Done. A bargain. Pack your bags, Reginald. Us girls are going on a road trip," said Ronnie.

Fat Susie frowned, perplexed.

I also frowned. "I'm still not happy."

"I know, but I want to do this. Helping these girls, it could be therapeutic. Do you think?"

I turned to the two body guards in rocking chairs.

"Fat Susie."

"Yessir."

"You will shoot first if you see anyone I hate. I'll give you a list."

"Sho'nuff," he said.

"You guys go eat. I think Manny's got it about ready. Something healthy, like kale and organic water."

Carlos and Fat Susie stood and went through the door. Carlos mumbled something about bringing their own burritos and margaritas next time and Fat Susie mumbled something about hell yeah.

I asked Ronnie, "When do you leave?"

"Tonight, after dinner. I'm already packed. We'll swing by Reginald's home and collect his things. I should only be gone a couple days. When is your meeting with the local scum and villainy?"

"Soon."

The screen door opened behind me. Though it was hard to tell because of her discolored skin, Ronnie's face paled.

"Mack, your house is perfect!" called Candice Hamilton. "Like it was designed and decorated by one of those HGTV shows, you know the kind I mean? And this cocktail your roommate made... Oh, pardon me, I didn't see your company."

"That's okay...I'm just leaving," said Ronnie. Her voice was weak.

"Alright. Hurry up, Mack, I'm famished!" said Candice and I heard her retreat back into the house.

Ronnie turned and walked unsteadily towards her car.

"Ronnie," I said.

"I'm going for some...food. Take out. Chinese, maybe."

She got to her red Mercedes and fumbled with her keys.

"I'm okay," she said. "Who is she? No, don't disclose that. Seeing her was a surprise, that's all."

She was scratching the paint with her keys. I placed my hand on hers. She trembled.

"It's not locked," I said.

"I can't make my hands work." She kind of laughed. "I don't have any right to be jealous, Mackenzie. I know that."

"True."

"It's just...every time I park at this house I know I don't belong. And a girl like her, she does. And she's so pretty, and I know I can't keep you."

"Relax," I said. "Take deep breaths. You're stronger than this. I'm right here."

"You're the only good person I've ever met, the only good person who sees me, or is trying to, and I'm ruining it."

I squeezed her hand. "That's Candice Hamilton. A defense attorney from northern Virginia. We're working together. We're colleagues."

"You don't need to explain. I don't deserve it. I know I don't, not yet. It was just the shock of her walking out of your door." She was talking as if from a trance, staring hard at her hands. "I can't breathe. I don't know what to do because I feel like I'm drowning, or you're drowning, or Kix is drowning, and I don't know how to save any of us and I'm running out of time and oxygen."

"That's fear and abuse and abandonment talking. It's messing with you. Which is nothing to be ashamed of. You've earned the right to struggle through a few abandonment issues."

"Shit, I'm pathetic." She wiped at her eyes. "You've put up with so many surprises of mine and you never cried."

"Balderdash. I cried."

She went a little limp and leaned against me. "That woman is pretty and she's the type of girl who deserves you and I want you to be happy. Did you really cry over me?"

"Of course I cried. I'm smitten with you," I said. And I squeezed her hand, which still held the keys.

"Ugh. I'm a mess. I can do this, Mackenzie. I promise. I can get to a point where you being near another woman won't send me into a tailspin. If you'd warned me beforehand..."

"That makes sense. You've been through a lot."

"Damn it, she's cute and my face is destroyed." She wiped more at her cheeks. "And she's already acting so fucking proprietary and intimate towards you."

I laughed.

"She's lonely and a little needy," I said.

"I won't kill her. I promise."

"Good to know. Baby steps."

The screen door opened again. Fat Susie, looking unhappy.

Ronnie took a shaky breath, then another, and called, "Let's go, Reginald. I'll get us burgers or chicken or Chinese or something."

"Good," he said, coming down the stairs. He moved well for a big guy. "Manny only got salads in there."

Ronnie put her free hand flat on my chest and pushed, getting herself a little space.

"I'm fine. I promise I am," she said.

"Fine as hell," I agreed.

"I'm serious. It doesn't look like it, but I'm much healthier than I was months ago."

"Yeah but your face is purple," I said.

"I'm not jealous. I don't get jealous. That's not something I get to be, after what I put you through."

"Okay."

"But if you sleep with her, I'm going to key your car. And have sex with everyone you know. And send you the photos."

I squeezed her hand a final time. "Not sure those are baby steps."

She smiled. "You're in love with a train wreck and she expresses affection through irrational covetousness."

"I never said I'm in love with you."

"Maybe do a better job of picking whom you fall for, Mackenzie. But not her. Please."

"Fat Susie," I said. "I'm serious. You see Darren Robbins or Toby or anyone, you fire your weapon. If you see them, they're coming for Ronnie and they'll kill you too."

"You got it, white man."

Ronnie kissed my check and opened her car door.

"Ronnie," I said.

"Yes Mackenzie."

"Stay safe."

"You got it, white man," she said.

20

"I need to prove Grady Huff had feelings for Juanita Yates," I told Kix at the breakfast table. "And that his romantic notions were reciprocated."

I don't care, said Kix.

Then he proclaimed something enthusiastically about his Cheerios and ate one, carefully guiding it into his mouth.

I drank some coffee.

"But I don't know how to prove that."

Where's the blonde lady? I miss her. She always kisses my face. The other woman, she was too preoccupied with herself and her heinous daughter.

"So you know what I'm going to do?" I said.

Put some chocolate syrup into my milk?

"I'm going to pester people."

Kix raised his milk.

What a coincidence. Those are my plans today too.

~

Claytor Lake was smaller than Smith Mountain Lake and the houses perched on the shoreline less expensive. With enough digging, however, gold could be found in them there hills, and it was to those more affluent neighborhoods that I steered.

The day was gray and moisture hung in the air like a veil. The lake sat smugly at two thousand feet above sea level and it held onto the chill.

To complete the disguise of classy and erudite gentleman, I wore my overcoat and jaunty herringbone cap and driving gloves. I knocked on ten doors off Cedar Point, near Ms. Yates's small brick ranch. I showed the six people who answered a photograph of Juanita Yates and asked, "Do you know this woman?"

They did not.

I followed with a second question, "Do any of your neighbors have their house cleaned professionally by a young Hispanic girl?"

The first five people did not.

The final woman glared and closed the door.

No dice.

I drove to another affluent neighborhood, farther away from Ms. Yates and repeated the process. These houses were stately and colonial, newer construction off Cardinal.

The first lady, middle-aged, a little chubby in the neck, short bob haircut, flowery shirt, said, "Yes? Do I know you?"

I raised the photograph. "Apologies for the intrusion. I'm looking for this girl. Do you know her?"

"I'm sorry, sir, I don't." She made ready to close the door, clearly overwhelmed with my genteel smile.

"She was a cleaning lady. Maybe if your neighbors—"

"You know," she said, interrupting me. "Now that you

mention it, that girl looks like the Mexican woman I've seen driving around. But in the photo, she's younger."

"Mexican."

"One of them places down south," she said and she closed the door.

I knocked at her neighbor's.

A man answered, less decorous than me. He looked about seventy but still fit. He had a good tan for his age, and a lot of silver hair. Gold chain around his neck. It wasn't noon yet but he had a White Russian in his left fist.

I showed him the photograph.

"Maybe I know her," he said, looking from the photograph and back. "Why you asking?"

"She was murdered several months ago."

The man hooted, "Murdered!" He threw open the door and stepped aside. "God almighty, that's why she quit showing up!"

I went in, out of the chill, and he closed the door. We remained in his foyer, tastefully decorated with nude paintings of women. Plus a tasteful marble statue of a woman who was nude and happy about it.

"You're kind of a big fellow, huh?" he asked.

"I gotta be. I'm compensating."

"For what?"

"I don't have pornography in my foyer," I said. "And I feel rotten about it. So this girl, did she clean your house?"

"She had just started. Less I miss my guess, that's Carlotta."

"Carlotta," I repeated.

Ah hah! A clue. She used different names. Less inspectors might've missed it, but not me and my jaunty cap.

Elementary, my dear Watson.

He said, "Right, Carlotta. Sweet girl, with an ass like a

butterball ham. A friend recommended her. But after her second cleaning she vanished. I suppose she went and got herself killed, huh."

I pretended to make a note in my phone.

"Sweet girl...ass like...a...butterball...ham. Got it."

He looked mildly alarmed.

I said, "Who recommended her?"

"Hey now, just a damn second. Are you looking for her killer? I'll guaran-damn-tee you it wasn't my pal."

"We already know who killed her," I said. "The guy confessed."

"The killer confessed? What kinda nut job...don't he watch cop shows? Never confess!"

"Right? What an idiot. Can I get the name and number?"

"Hell, I'll do better than that. He's my next-door neighbor. Or he was. His wife still lives there. She can tell you where he is, the rascal, though he shows up here now and then."

He marched out in flip-flops and started across his damp front lawn.

"You in the market for a boat?" he asked over his shoulder.

"I am not."

"Make you a good deal. I got dozens."

"Do you have speed boats?"

"Sure I got speed boats!" he said.

"I hate speed boats."

He turned enough to squint at me, look me up and down, and kept going.

The neighbor's house was built into the side of a hill, above the water. The front was only one story, but the land fell away in the back and exposed three stories. There was a metaphor in there somewhere...

He banged on the green slab door and shouted. “Sally! You home?” He tried the knob. “Sally!”

A minute later a woman answered. Maybe forty-five and severe, her eyes sharp and cut at us unhappily. Black turtleneck, black slacks.

“George, you know I don’t like when you shout. What business do you have over here? None that I can imagine,” she said. “Who’s this, who’s your friend?”

“Carlotta got herself murdered!” hooted George the speed boat salesman. “You believe it?”

“I have nothing to say about that girl.”

“God almighty, murdered. I had wondered where she ran off to.”

I tipped my cap to the woman. “Mackenzie August, ma’am. Carlotta was murdered and her killer is in custody. I’m doing some follow-up questioning.”

“I’m sure I don’t know how I could help.”

“Can we talk? Five minutes,” I said.

“You’re with the police?”

“Franklin County sheriff’s office.”

It was mostly true.

She made a little shooing motion. “Run on home, George. I’ll speak with your friend. Run on.”

“I’ll be damned,” he said, turning towards home. “Cute as can be, that Carlotta. Who’d want to kill her?”

Sally let me in. She closed the door and locked it. We sat on white wicker chairs near a coat stand. All the rooms I could see were sparsely decorated—plain and serious, like the owner.

“That George, banging on my door every few days, always with a cocktail.”

I showed her the photograph.

“Look familiar?”

"Yes," she said. "That's Carlotta, plain as day. She used to clean our house."

"And then one day about six months ago she quit showing up?"

She arched a thin and imperial eyebrow. "Oh no. I ran her off before then. She tried to get fresh with my husband."

Ah hah! A romantic tryst with a second client. So it wasn't just Grady Huff.

Had Juanita/Carlotta been so irresistibly nubile and vulnerable that every male client was destined to fall for her? Or was something more disquieting and baleful at play?

I pushed my cap backwards and whistled.

"Is that so."

"Surely is. I ran her off and then a couple weeks later I threw him out too. Got so I couldn't stand the sight of him," she said.

"Your husband."

She had a way of speaking, with her head cocked, that lent her righteous indignation. Like a disgruntled southern baptist preacher.

"Alvin, yes. He's still pals with George and he comes banging on my door asking for forgiveness every few days."

"How'd you know Carlotta tried to get fresh with Alvin?" I asked.

"I saw it with my own two eyes. At the boat dock."

At the boat dock. Which is where Grady Huff had shot her, at his own dock.

"How'd she take the news, when you fired her?"

"Well, I suppose, it wasn't all her fault. George, he's a philanderer. Been caught half a dozen times with his pants down. Carlotta, she handled it as a girl ought. She struck me as contrite and mortified. Left without complaint."

"How old is Alvin?"

"Fifty-one."

"And you believe Carlotta, a cute twenty-five year-old, was desirous of him?"

"Alvin," she said with a faint smile. "He's always been a charmer. He has his ways."

"That Alvin sounds like a rascal."

"Surely is."

"Where'd you learn about Carlotta's housekeeping services? A reference?"

"You'd have to ask him. Alvin, I mean."

"Where can I find him?" I asked.

"A bar, probably."

"You have his number?"

"I suppose I do," she said.

I STOPPED at a gas station in Radford to fill up my shiny spaceship and took the onramp north towards Roanoke.

After a few miles I realized the same black sedan that'd followed me into the gas station was hanging off my tail at a distance of a quarter mile.

A coincidence?

I slowed.

After a half minute delay during which the gap between us shrank, the black sedan slowed too.

"Zounds," I said. "Evil doers."

I slowed further, dropping to forty-five and hoping to get a glimpse of the plate number, but the pursuing criminal masterminds kept their distance.

"I need a crime-fighting canine companion," I told

myself. "To whom I could make pithy and laconic jokes about situations such as these."

The cosmos did not reply.

Exit 141 came over the hill and I gunned the engine. I took the pretzel offramp at sixty-five, executed a highly illegal and highly sexy maneuver which involved running the stop sign, cutting through traffic on 419, nearly causing an accident, and hiding in the parking lot at the LaQuinta Inn.

And I lay in-wait within the crowded lot and my own smuggery.

Twenty-seconds later the black sedan rushed to the stop sign and braked hard enough to squeal the tires. From the distance, I couldn't make out the plate but discerned there were multiple villains within the sedan. The sedan waited. And waited some more, to the frustration of the cars piling behind.

"Where'd I go?" I wondered on their behalf. "How'd I get away so quickly? Raw skill? Supernatural driving ability?"

They had to be goons hired by Darren Robbins, that no-good-dirty-rotten-pig-stealing hack of a prosecutor, the ex-fiancé of the girl of my dreams.

The car behind my pursuers, tired of waiting, honked.

The sedan burnt the tires, spun in a circle, cut across the oncoming traffic, and raced down the northbound ramp and fled into the distance. Sensing a trap, perhaps.

I tried to follow but at the poignant moment in time an elderly couple stepped in front of my car, on the way to theirs. She moved slowly and her doting husband stayed with her, hand under her left arm. Their progress was discernible but only just. They reached the far side and she noticed me in the driver's seat. She raised up a little bit, smiled, and waved.

I debated running them over.

Or explaining to them that their advanced age had spoiled my fool-proof snare.

But they had charmed me. And one day in the future I hoped to be helping the love of my life to our car, and I'd rather a young and shockingly attractive man not run us over.

So I waved back.

21

Tuesday afternoon I was driving to meet Alvin at All-Sports Cafe when Marcus Morgan called.

"August, you got your meeting," he said. "A meeting of the muscle and the minds. Over a game of poker."

"Atta boy, Marcus."

"You 'atta boy' me again, I break your right knee cap."

"But that's the leg I use for the gas pedal. And of tantamount importance, the brake," I said.

"Meeting is Saturday night."

"That's forever."

"I asked him to lay off you til then. Cashed in some credit. Toby's another story, though. Darren wanted Friday but we got our first playoff game that night," said Marcus.

"We? You playing?"

"No. My son is, you know this. And I live vicariously."

"When you're on speaker phone, your voice loses some of it's gravel. You're less Idris Elba and more Steve Urkel," I said.

"Now I think about it, I hope Darren shoots you in the ear."

He hung up.

ALL-SPORTS WAS your typical local bar—designed on a budget with no real theme other than loud paint and a panoply of televisions. Drop ceiling, black chairs and stools, shiny tables, framed sports pictures, pendants, jerseys, that kind of place.

Alvin stood from the bar to shake my hand.

"Mackenzie?"

"That's me."

"Alvin Bradley."

Alvin was thick around the middle, the face, and every where else. He had a full head of hair and decent brown beard. Open face, eyes maybe too closely set, and he wore a Coors Light rain jacket.

I signaled the bartender and he wandered over.

Alvin said, "Keith, this is Mackenzie. Put his on my tab. As long as he's drinking Miller."

"I'll have a Coors Banquet, Keith," I said.

Keith acquiesced and brought me one and a napkin.

I drank some.

I said, "You move beer for Miller?"

"Regional manager," said Alvin. "All Miller products as well as the local stuff. You wouldn't believe how much beer this country puts away."

"May God continue to bless the United States."

Alvin raised his glass. "I'll drink to that."

"I met Sally."

"My wife. How'd she look?"

"Stolid," I said.

"Maybe use a smaller word, guy. I sell beer."

"She misses you, though she's reticent to admit it, I think. The only time she smiled was the occasion she mentioned your charm."

"Sal tell you we're estranged?"

"It came up. But that's not why I'm here," I said.

"I miss her. God, I do. But you could say I'm getting what I deserve."

"Did Sally phone you about Carlotta?"

"Carlotta? What about her? Sal and I ain't spoke a couple weeks," he said.

"Carlotta's dead. Murdered."

His beer paused halfway to his mouth. He set it down on the napkin and sat up a little straighter.

"Murdered."

"As a doornail," I said.

"I didn't do it."

"I know. The guy confessed."

"Murdered. Well hell. Not every day you know somebody who got killed."

"Yeah it's one of those big deals in life. You'll feel unsettled a few days."

Keith the bartender brought nachos. Alvin slid the plate between us and nodded at them.

"How'd she...I mean, who killed her?"

"One of her clients. She cleaned his house."

Alvin's face, the part I could see around his beard, was a little white.

"Jesus," he said.

"I'm trying to suss out a motive. Be nice if you could tell me your story and how you acquired her services."

"Sure," he said. He took a swallow of beer. Then another, draining the glass. Wiped his mouth and signaled Keith for a refill. "Sure, I'll help. Damn. Okay."

"Anything you say stays between us."

"Carlotta and me, we were screwing around," said Alvin. "You knew? Sal caught us."

"Who instigated the romance?"

"Me, I guess. But, you know, Mack, I've thought about this some. I put the moves on her, right? But...damned if she wasn't putting signals out too. I got so I can recognize the signals a woman gives, and Carlotta was putting them out."

"Tell me about the signals."

"She would smile at me. Watch me, when we were both there. Long eye contact. She'd look at me the way a woman does, you know the look? So, one time...damn it, I'm not proud of this. I arranged for Sal to be out of the house when Carlotta came to clean. Just to see what would happen. And it happened. Anyway, now she's dead and I don't want to talk bad about the dead. But her outfit was different that day. Like she was the maid in a sleazy movie. Like she'd been waiting to wear it. One thing led to another."

"Sounds to me like she seduced you, rather than the other way round," I said.

"I think maybe she did. That don't make what I did right, though."

"How long did this go on?"

"Not long," he said. Keith put another beer down and Alvin ate a few nacho chips. "Not long. One day she wanted to go swimming at the dock. She started undressing but that's when Sal came home. Unexpectedly, right? You can imagine that shit hitting the fan."

I could. And I wouldn't want to get on the wrong side of Sally's wrath. Not with that severe turtleneck.

Alvin had none of the charm or charisma intimated by Sally. He was a couple years beyond middle-aged, overweight, a middle manager who sold beer and who seemed to have no sexual appeal about him.

Even curiouser for Carlotta to hit on him.

"I moved out soon after," said Alvin. "I mean, Sal threw me out. I texted Carlotta but she never replied."

"Never heard from her again?"

"No." He smiled without humor and chuckled. "Not directly."

"Not directly," I repeated.

"Her brothers came calling on me at work."

"Carlotta has brothers?"

"Apparently." He chuckled again. Sounded like he smoked. "Two of them. Big guys, kinda scary. Mexican or whatever Carlotta was. Said their sister got fired because of me and I should be ashamed and her reputation was ruined and blah blah."

"Kind of like protecting their sister's honor?"

"Maybe. Mostly, though, they wanted money. Said Carlotta should be compensated financially until she found more work," said Alvin.

Hmmmmmm, I thought.

"Hmmmmm," I said.

"Yeah."

"It's peculiar Carlotta didn't come to you herself. If she'd been interested in you, now that you were single why not arrange to meet you again?"

He stroked his beard and stared absently at the television.

"That's a good question. I never thought about it exactly like that, I was so broke up over Sal. Good damn question, Mackenzie. Why didn't she come herself? Did she like me or not?"

"Maybe her affection was illusory?"

"Huh."

"What'd you tell the two brothers?" I asked.

"I told them to get the hell out of my warehouse or I'd call the guys. And I had a lot of big guys there. The brothers left but told me they'd be back."

"Did they?"

"No," he said. "Never heard from them or Carlotta again. Probably because she got herself killed. Who'd you say it was? Another client?"

"Yes. Although she was using a different name. Called herself Juanita Yates."

"Is that so? Well damn. I got no idea what to think."

"Do you know where she lived?" I asked.

"Got no idea."

"What'd she drive?"

"Jeep Cherokee," he said.

"How many other clients did she have?"

"No clue. Sorry."

"Did she ever tell you anything about herself?" I asked.

"No, there wasn't much talking. Before or...after."

"History, family, likes, dislikes, other jobs?"

"Nope. I'm not much help, huh."

"How'd you find her?"

"My buddy. Said he found her on Craigslist. How about I get you his info?" said Alvin.

"Sure," I said.

"So if the killer confessed, what's all this matter?"

"I want to know," I said, "what exactly happened the day she died. It doesn't make sense. So I'm trying to determine motive. And I hate the opposing counsel."

22

I did the dishes Wednesday night because Manny had cooked dinner—salmon in tinfoil boats with butter and lemon and asparagus.

Mi casa es su casa.

Timothy August and Sheriff Stackhouse settled onto the leather couch to watch some indie movie that was winning awards. From my spot in the kitchen I had a clear view of them. He put his arm around her shoulders and she leaned against him.

Manny nudged me and indicated them with his chin.

"Those two. That's the best, sí?"

"My old man and the sheriff?"

"*Simon*," he said. "That romance, it makes me happy."

I finished washing and dried my hands with a towel.

"What are we doing tonight?" he asked.

"Something dissimilar to the lovebirds on the couch."

"Put Kix to bed, señor. You and me, we'll go to the gym. You are getting fat."

"Am not. I went last week."

"Only once to the gym? Dios mio. What is a giant American word for fat? One of those big stupid words you use?" he said.

"Corpulent."

"*Sí, bueno*. You are corpulent." He pulled up his polo shirt and flexed abdominal muscles. A thin guy naturally with narrow hips, his torso had muscles etched just below his skin, like a professional athlete. Was I so inclined, I'd swoon. "Look, migo. You see this? No carbs."

I pulled up my shirt. I had a few lines showing, but not like I once did. I flexed harder but no additional muscular definition surged into view.

"You put on weight?" he asked.

"No. Yes. Shut up. A few pounds."

"You have…a three-pack, maybe. Get your gloves."

"Gloves," I said.

"Sí. The dojo."

"Good idea. Let's hit things. Like your face with my fat hands."

He shot me a thumbs up. "That's the spirit, big Mack. Corpulent Mack."

MANNY and I frequented a local martial arts club to work-out. The club met twice a week after-hours in a karate academy and it was specifically for more serious fighters, often competing in events like Spartyka.

A couple older guys, this was their passion. They arrived early to set up the mats and two makeshift rings, and they stayed late to clean and mop. During the training they'd shout instructions to younger idiots.

Like Manny.

Big Will and a couple of his enormously-biceped

comrades were jumping rope in the corner. Then they'd drop the rope and work the chin-up bar. Big Will wore his standard red hoodie, slowly soaking through. He nodded at us by jerking his chin our way, which was the brawniest way to do it. He looked a little like James Harden, I thought.

Manny and I alternated hitting a speed bag and heavy bag until it was our turn in one of the rings. I ducked under the top rope and tightened my training gloves while Manny went for water.

"Here he is. Here's the gumshoe thinks he's funny."

Toby Moreno had entered the dojo, along with Dexter. I knew Toby from a meeting over the summer—Don Draper-looking guy, professional hitman. Elite muscle for the District Kings. Marcus respected him, which carried water in my book.

With him was Dexter, Darren Robbin's shadow. Black guy, thin, shaved head. He wore a blue sports jacket hiding a shoulder rig and pistol.

Marcus Morgan had warned me—Toby might not wait for the Saturday night convening. And here he came with a gunner.

"Watch your mouth, Toby," I said. "I'm hilarious."

He pointed at my gloves. "You know how to use those things?"

"Only to open cans of pickles, with the lid on too tight." I walked their way and rested my hands on the ropes.

Why did I walk their way? To send an immediate message—I'm not afraid and I don't run. Who was the message for? Mostly myself.

I asked, "Thrown anybody off a rooftop recently?"

"That guy? That guy got off easy compared to what's coming to you."

"Certainly your master, Darren Robbins, didn't send you

into a dojo full of fighters to cause trouble. Not even he's that stupid."

Dexter remained stoic.

Toby's face turned a little red. "Darren ain't my boss, asshole."

"Sure he is. That's why you're here. You're an errand boy. Albeit, one with great hair."

Big Will had stopped his routine, watching us with interest. If the balloon went up, whose side was he on?

Probably not mine. He'd shot at me before with a shotgun. Dead giveaway.

"Told you before," said Toby. "You ought be tied to concrete and tossed in Smith Mountain. Be doing everyone a favor."

"That's why you're in Roanoke, like a good lapdog. Calvin Summers is dead. Plus his daughter dumped your boss. So Darren snapped and you came running. Sit, Toby, sit."

Toby said, "Keep talking, big guy. You're dead, you just don't know it."

"Is your hair gel responsibly sourced from renewable materials? I'm worried it's petroleum based," I said. "Bad, Toby, bad."

"Dexter, maybe you put one through this guy's right eye and we go home," said Toby. "We'd get out of this pathetic dojo easy enough."

Dexter did a shrug and reached inside his jacket.

But, as if by magic, the barrel of Manny's pistol pressed firmly into Dexter's back. Dexter froze.

"These two ass clowns," said Manny. "Dos pendejos. Can't even watch their six. Watch their six, I say that right?"

Dexter, a calm and stoic man by nature, looked downright forlorn. A gun muzzle will do that.

Toby didn't move, other than to nod slowly. "I get it. I see this. You brought your boyfriend. I heard about this guy. Let me guess. Manny the corrupt marshal."

"You move," said Manny. "And I wreck your lower spine with my .357, migo."

Manny reached around and removed the Glock from Dexter's shoulder rig. Handed it to one of the old boxing coaches, watching this interaction with alarm. The old guy took it but he wasn't happy. Then Manny lifted the pistol from the small of Toby's back. It'd been tucked under his belt and I didn't see what kind. Toby was smart enough not to object.

The old guy said, "I need to call the police?"

"I the police," said Manny. "Federal marshal. We all good, señor."

"You two sonofabitches are making a colossal mistake," said Toby.

"I've been making those for months."

"Years, *pana*," Manny corrected me. He gave Toby a shove. "You, good-looking guy. You are Italian? The Italian stallion? Get in the ring."

"Get in the ring," said Toby.

"Pronto."

"You want me to fight your boyfriend? I do this for a living, marshal. I'll kill the guy," said Toby. He hadn't taken his eyes off me.

A little haunting, to be honest.

"I want you to kill him," said Manny.

"You sure?"

"Sí, baby."

"Sí, baby," I agreed. "Show me how the gloves work. Kill, Toby, kill."

"I got your word, I break his face," said Toby, "and you don't shoot."

"Got my word," said Manny. By now we'd drawn a crowd. Tension will do that. And Manny's gun was gasoline on the fire. "Everybody hear? I am a federal marshal. I won't shoot. My word."

"Good hell, a couple of idiots, you are," said Toby. He stepped out of his leather loafers and ducked under the top rope. He hadn't worn exercise gear but his outfit wasn't untenable—his pants were loose linen and his shirt was stretchy long-sleeved cotton, no collar. "I'll do this for free. No one needs to pay me a dime."

"Violence is its own reward?" I said.

Manny tossed Toby his pair of training gloves.

"Don't get Mack's blood on them, *por favor*."

I nodded at the old guy operating the bell and timer. "Three rounds. Five minutes each."

Dexter made a snickering sound. "Bitch, need for round two, my guess."

That didn't bode well for me.

Maybe Manny should shoot them instead.

I was barefoot and I began some light hopping, transferring weight one foot to the other.

Was I a betting man, I wouldn't know where to place my money. Toby hurt people as a career. However I used to fight in cage matches in Los Angeles. Toby might be in better shape but I had a couple inches and twenty pounds on him. A bad loss was within the realm of probability.

So why was I fighting? Good question. Maybe someone smarter could tell me.

It had something to do with pride. Something to do with genitalia comparison. But more than that, it had to do with

Ronnie. She'd stood up to these guys. She'd taken their punches and survived. So I could too.

If I couldn't, I didn't deserve her.

And if I didn't fight him now, Toby would know he'd won. And he'd kill me soon. So it was about Ronnie but also about survival.

Big Will caught my eye. He stood behind Dexter, arms crossed, and he gave me a slow nod. Maybe he didn't like these big swinging dicks coming to town and threatening everyone either. I was the lesser of two pains in the ass.

The crowd around the ring was three people deep in places. They knew. Something wicked was afoot.

The bell rang.

Toby came out in a closed boxing stance. Fists balled near his face.

I did a little more hopping, moving around the ring away from him, shaking my hands a little. Sweating.

"Get off your bicycle, piece of shit," said Toby. "This won't hurt long."

He closed.

I dropped into a shallow squat, a forward stance.

Because it was the only kind I'd ever learned.

He threw a right and I understood immediately that I was gonna win, if I didn't make a mistake.

He should have led with some probing jabs using his left hand. See what I could do with them, see if I was any good, discover who was quicker. But instead he gathered behind his right hand. Put all his weight into it, trying to kill me with one shot. Swing for the fences. Powerful but slow. Pure arrogance.

I took his fist on the meaty part of my left shoulder, and it staggered me to the side. Painful but no damage done.

It made a good sound and he grinned with satisfaction.

Toby had never been trained. An experienced fighter never underestimates his opponent. Toby was tough and cruel and unafraid of violence and pain, but there'd been no rigorous practice behind it. He was the kind of guy who hurt people by intimidating and overpowering them. He'd break the hands of lesser men by squeezing. He'd smack them around because people would let him, even tougher guys. Toby was a bull. Bulls didn't need practice, they assumed.

But anyone watching who knew their stuff, they knew immediately he wasn't skilled.

He got behind another right hook, feeling smug.

My left hand darted out and smacked him. Kind of a jab, too quick for Toby.

I danced backwards and came in again, another smack.

He tried a right hook again—his tried and true bread and butter, never let him down before. But it missed and he stumbled.

He was off balance so I came with a flurry of slaps. One, two, three, hard hands to the skull that stung.

The crowd laughed.

Why slaps? Because I wanted him embarrassed.

His face began to swell from open-handed impacts.

Like Ronnie's had.

He wasn't a mixed martial arts fighter, he was a brawler. No, he wasn't even that—he was a puncher. Powerful but inaccurate.

Toby lunged suddenly and fought like mad. Short crisp shots I absorbed on my arms and shoulders. He was strong and my body would ache tomorrow.

I raised up my right knee, got my foot into his chest, and did a front push kick. Like a battering ram. He was thrown backwards hard enough to land on his neck.

The crowd loved it.

"Down goes Toby," I said, like Howard Cosell. "Down goes Toby."

He grunted.

Manny clapped Dexter on the shoulder.

I panted. Toby was gasping.

"Fight's over," I said. "As soon as you surrender."

I could have landed on him. He didn't know a thing about mat work. But that wasn't sexy.

He got to his feet and said, "Fuck you," dragging out the F sound.

I took control of the match. Closed the distance and began hammering him. He wanted to counter but I kept circling to his left, away from the one arrow in his quiver, the big right. He didn't know what to do with my kicks and soon he hurt everywhere. He landed a good kidney punch, powerful enough to fracture ribs, and one shot to my ear that hurt like hell.

But soon he was bleeding from the mouth, nose, and eyes. He moved heavily, holding his side, and tried to stay away from me. After four minutes he had no oxygen and couldn't keep his hands up.

"You're a thug, Toby," I told him between wheezes. "Not a fighter."

I hit him one final right cross and he dropped to his knees. Dazed. Probably a concussion.

"Sit, Toby, sit."

My hands hurt. I should've ended him. That was the point of fighting like this. Knock out or force a submission.

But I stayed back, feeling good and dancing on the balls of my feet. Besides, I was a pacifist. Sorta. Jesus never punched guys in the head.

Toby had trouble focusing. Couldn't get up.

A couple of the old guys, the patriarchs of the MMA

club, came into the ring waving their hands. The bell clanged. Fight was over. A technical knock out.

"Get back," said Toby, but it sounded like "Gebbag." He tried to push them aside but had no muscle power.

I went to the ropes and Manny gave me water.

Big Will nodded approval and went back to his jump rope.

I told Dexter, "Your boy didn't last one round."

Dexter refused to speak, the sore loser.

"If you tell Darren Robbins about this," I said between deep breaths. "Can you make it so we're in a dark alley? And I'm shirtless? And wearing a fedora? That would paint a more dramatic visual in Darren's mind, I think."

Manny grinned and squeezed Dexter's shoulder in a kind of side hug.

"And me," said Manny. "I want to be wearing a cowboy hat and drinking a margarita. With a pretty señorita who got ass. This okay? When you tell your *jefe*?"

Dexter glared murder.

23

Kix and I were spending the morning together. We ate a lazy breakfast and watched Sesame Street and knocked over towers of blocks. Afterwards I set him on the floor of my bedroom while I examined myself in the mirror, shirtless.

My ribs ached when I inhaled and they were a dark purple. The contusion was near a scar I earned during a knife fight with a guy named Silva last year. Also my ear was bruised where the pinna connected to the skull—hopefully no cauliflower cartilage would manifest. I had an appearance to maintain.

Stupid Toby.

Kix watched me curiously and without judgement. Which was meritorious of him.

I was applying a dab of Neosporin when Ronnie called. I put her on speaker.

"Hello Mackenzie. I'm taking you to dinner tonight."

"In Virginia Beach?"

She said, "I'm driving to Roanoke this afternoon, leading a caravan of girls caught in human trafficking. Did you know we have something in Roanoke called Street Ransom that assists at-risk women? Provides them with a place to stay. Who knew. I might give them gobs of money."

"I did not know this."

"I return to the beach tomorrow morning, but that provides you ample time to wine and dine me this evening. I promise to be pliable and willing and contributory," she said.

"It's a date."

"That gives me tingles. A real date?"

"I'll wear cologne and a sports jacket."

"Not for long."

I GOT to Frankie Rowlands at 6:30pm

Ronnie arrived eleven minutes later, preceded by Fat Susie. There was no gasp from the bar when she walked in, but rather the opposite—the noise level diminished. A naturally breath-taking woman in the prime of her life, in peak physical condition, in heels and a form-fitting crimson dress and iridescent diamonds, and her honey hair in an updo... well, that was worth pausing to admire.

And so I did.

Along with everyone else.

"Mackenzie," she said.

"Sun goddess," I replied. Fat Susie and I shook hands and I said, "Thanks for bringing her home safe."

"I ain't do much. Your girl can kick ass."

"Thank you, Reginald. Wait at the bar?" she said.

He complied.

The hostess took us to our table, one with a white tablecloth and candle. Frankie Rowlands was the kind of place you only went if you had three hundred dollars to blow before dessert and you limited yourself to one libation. The walls were genuine wood, the paintings were original, and the snootiness was authentic.

She smiled at Ronnie and whispered, "Your dress is heavenly," and left.

I got Ronnie's chair and she said, "Do you like it?"

"Your celestial dress? I am aggressively fond of it. Is it new?"

"Purchased not an hour ago, from PS Freedom. I changed in the boutique's dressing room," she said.

"I might call you a thing divine, for nothing natural I ever saw so noble."

"Are you quoting a poem?"

"Yes but botching it," I said and I sat across from her.

"As long as you insinuate I'm ravishing."

"That and every other superlative I can fathom."

I ordered an Old Fashioned and she ordered a pineapple martini, and when the drinks came the couple at the adjacent table raised their glasses in toast. They looked seventy-ish and had the air of money about them.

The man said, "You two are damned attractive. God bless you."

I lifted my drink to him.

The woman told Ronnie, "You, dear, are as pretty as old women like me pretend we used to be."

Ronnie smiled at her (despite being in the periphery, I was nearly melted) and said, "You're the sweetest, thank you. This is our first official date, although I've been after him for over a year. Wish me luck."

The woman glowered at me. "If tonight doesn't go well, you're a fool."

"A damned fool," her husband agreed.

"So much pressure. Now I'm nervous."

"Don't be," said Ronnie. "I'm a foregone conclusion."

Human beings can't glow. But I swore she intensified the purity of color in the room.

Our salads came and she told me about her time at the beach, finding the mistreated girls and locating safe shelters for them. It involved barging into a senator's office in Richmond.

I regaled her with my last few days, and she lowered her fork to her salad plate.

She asked, "You fought Toby? Toby Moreno."

"I did."

"Why?"

"Good question. He showed up looking for trouble," I said.

"You won?"

"That's a tad insulting."

She finished her drink and set it down. She leaned backwards and watched me. I, on the other hand, didn't know where to look, with her bright eyes, sparkling earrings, cami straps and plunging neckline. She said, "You beat Toby Moreno in a fight."

"Naturally."

"I don't understand you. Sometimes I think I do, but... who or what are you, Mackenzie? Toby is elite. One of the world's true scary guys. He kills people."

The lady at the adjacent table made a soft gasp.

I believe she was eavesdropping, the nosey nellie.

Ronnie didn't detect the spy or didn't care. "Television shows about organized crime, like Sopranos or The Wire. They're based around Toby, or people like him. He's an enforcer. And you beat him?"

I shrugged modestly.

"He took his victory for granted. Made him over-confident."

"You have no bruises or marks, at least not on your face," she said.

"He mostly hit my arms. Bad aim, the nincompoop. My ear hurts, though."

"That means you're the best of the best. At...what, violence? Sometimes I think you're this gentle giant who wouldn't hurt a fly and then...I remember you're scary."

"Strength of character can take the appearance of the capacity for destruction, which from a distance is scary."

Ronnie said, "You could make more money working for the underworld, Mackenzie."

"Maybe. But yuck."

"Because of your admiration for Jesus?"

"That's a big part of it. I need help sleeping at night as it is, without actively destroying my soul. I connect on a seismic level with God's command to Adam and Eve."

"Which was?"

"Go into the world and subdue it. Bring order to the chaos," I said. "Not the other way round."

The lady next to us cleared her throat and dabbed at her mouth with a napkin.

"Like your house on Windsor," said Ronnie. "Inside I always feel sheltered from chaos."

"By intention."

"What about law enforcement?"

"Tried it. Too many rules. Too many cell phones," I said. "Too many traffic tickets. And less money."

The server brought our food and asked if Ronnie would like another pineapple martini.

"Please," she said and her eyes twinkled at me. "I'm not much of a drinker. But some nights are worth celebrating."

"As are some dresses."

"And the girl in the dress?"

"Worth an entire festival of jubilee."

We tucked in, though she did it with class and aplomb.

My filet was worth celebrating too.

She asked, "When is your big convening with Marcus and Darren?"

"Saturday evening."

"Are you scared?"

"A little," I said. "More like impatient. After the hootenanny I'll be dead or you'll be free."

"I'm already free. Freer than I've ever felt. I've been calling certain former clients. Though I was forced into relationship with them, a handful were kind and they assumed certain truths which are false. They're being hurt and it's not their fault—it's Darren's. I'm cutting them loose personally. Ergo, my freedom."

"Ergo," I said. "I love good vocab on a woman."

She raised her second martini glass, now half empty, and said, "It's the pineapple. Whooooo, it's strong. And I'm a lightweight."

"What will you do about your personal clients?" I asked. "Those not foist upon you by Darren and your father."

She was no longer eating and her eyes were shinning a little stronger. Due to vodka and pineapple. "I don't know. I'm still novice at being a fully functional adult. Why would I cut off personal clients? I'm treated well. They're lonely and I make their life better. In function, I'm basically Mother Teresa."

"There's a fundamental difference in providing care for the infirm and providing your body for the, ah, horny."

She said, "Tell me the difference. I'm so lost in it all I truly can't pinpoint the issue."

"I have no authority or right to pontificate on the matter. I'm a newbie too."

"Please?"

"In my opinion, the body and spirit are not separate. By allowing other men your body, you're giving them access to your core. On some level, you two belong to each other."

"That makes sense. I think," she said. Her words weren't slurred but I could tell she had to work harder than usual. "I trust you on this entirely."

"How would you feel if I dated other women?"

"I would die."

"Do you see?"

"I'm not dating these men. It's a business transaction," she said and she finished the martini.

I said, "Not to them. You told me you act as their girlfriend. For a price."

"An extremely high price, Mackenzie. There are only two regulars. And one of the guys, he owns an NBA team."

"If you don't want to stop, then don't. I'm not asking you to," I said.

"Why aren't you asking me to? I feel like you should. But it might be the martini talking. Dammit, I should not have had so much. These are *strong*."

At the moment, as if choreographed, our server brought her another drink, which was I thought presumptuous.

"Oh I shouldn't," said Ronnie.

Our server said, "On the house. The manager tonight wishes you to know she believes you to be the most beautiful woman and the pair of you the most beautiful couple she's ever seen."

I stood corrected. Not presumptuous but rather perspicacious to a high degree.

"Okay," said Ronnie. "But only a little. To be polite."

The server nodded with severe appreciation and left.

"Tell me," she said. "Why haven't you asked me to stop? Shouldn't you?"

"Have you read Dostoevsky's *Letters from the Underground*?" I asked.

"Of course."

"Is that so?"

"No, Mackenzie," she said with kind of a half snort. "God, no one reads these things but you. But I'll listen and watch your lips as you explain it."

"In the story, there's a wretched man who wants to feel noble and so he promises to save a prostitute from her life of sin. She takes him at his word and shows up at his house. But he cannot save her. He was merely being self-righteous and selfish. It ruins them both even further."

She nodded, looking down at her drink. Some of her light had extinguished.

The lady beside us was no longer covertly eavesdropping; she was plainly staring open-mouthed our direction.

I said, "If I ask you to stop, I'm trying to fix you. Possibly against your will. And that cannot work. If I try to fix you, it will ruin you and ruin us. It'll make me feel superior, like I have the answers even though I don't. By comparison, it'll put you at a disadvantage, a false one. It won't work. So instead, I'll enjoy your company and accept you as you are."

"Accept me as a friend," she said and she stumbled over the word accept.

"Yes."

"I cannot possibly be friends with you. I'm mad about you. I think about us an embarrassing amount." Her third martini was half consumed and she pushed it my way. "Sheesh. Take this away. It's going to kill me."

I slid the cocktail glass to my side and tried it.

Wow. If angels could be drinks, they would be pineapple martinis.

"I'm getting emotional," she said.

"It's the alcohol."

"I know. This is why I don't drink. But don't you want to be with me?

I nodded. Reached out and took her hand.

"Very very much. I want you in every way, but I refuse to be with someone else's girlfriend, and I also won't be with someone on the condition they change. I'll take you as you are or not at all."

"And you chose not at all. But it's just sex." She said it like, "jussex."

"There's no such thing as just sex, in my experience. And not for me. I'm too big of a Ronnie fan for it ever to be just sex," I said.

The man at the adjacent table handed his wife a napkin and she dabbed her eyes.

Ronnie said, "I don't want a fan, Mackenzie. I'm lonely. Why the hell did I break up with my fiancé?"

"For your benefit, not mine. When your father sent his buddy into your bedroom when you were a teenager, something broke. You no longer see sex and relationships in a healthy light."

The woman gasped.

Ronnie squeezed my hand.

I said, "Also, Ronnie, I'm no trained clinical psychologist, but I have a theory. You grew up wondering why your father hated you, why you could never make him happy. But there are men you can make happy—happy enough that they provide for you. One of the reasons you're hesitant to break off these personal clients is because they provide a type of paternal approval, which you crave."

"That makes it sound sick."

"That makes it sound like you're a human."

"Shit, you're right. I truly need help," she said.

The couple beside us stood and left. The woman sobbed softly on her way out.

Ronnie stared at her drink and said, "I need to go. I think I might be sick."

"I'll take you home."

"No. Reginald will take me home," she said. She called him Reshinul. "You cannot because this doesn't count as a true date. I ruined it with pineapple martinis and by being a slut."

"Not ruined for me. I enjoyed it."

"Damn it, I was going to be the best first date you've ever had."

"You were wonderful tonight," I said.

"Oh...damn it," she said again. "Tonight's Thursday, isn't it. I'm supposed to read bedtime stories at the Rescue Mission. I forgot."

"Too late now."

She stood. And swayed.

I reached her before she fell. Together we walked towards the door and she executed an admirable impression of a sober person. Despite the alcohol and heels, she moved with grace and strength.

I stopped the server and said, "We need to be availed of the check."

"Your bill has been paid, sir," she said.

"The heck you say."

"By the nice couple who left recently. They said you two needed some extra love tonight, whatever that means, sir."

Ronnie buried her face into my shoulder and made a whimpering sound.

"Very good." I pressed a few big bills into the server's hand and moved towards the door.

Fat Susie joined us.

"Where we going," he said.

"My spare bedroom," I think.

"She drunk?"

"No! No'm fine."

"More like sodden," I said.

"What's the difference?" asked Fat Susie.

"Sodden makes you sound erudite."

We got Ronnie outside, where she threw up.

24

Friday morning bright and early I pulled into the miniature mountain range that was the macadam parking lot of Western Virginia Regional Jail.

I checked my gun, said hello to the same unhappy guards, and sat in the odoriferous conference room.

Grady Huff soon shuffled in, dressed in a fashionable orange jumpsuit and the season's hottest cuffs.

"I figured out who you remind me of," I said. "Did you ever see *Toy Story 2*? Remember the toy collector, the guy with glasses and goatee?"

"Shut up, *fatty*. Where's Candice?" said Grady Huff.

"Too busy to be bothered, trying to save your ass. I'm meeting her for lunch, though, and I'll convey your warmest salutations."

"I got an idea. Put me on the stand. I'll tell my story to those poor saps and be scot free."

"But you said," I reminded him, "that jurors would hate you because you're rich."

"Whatever, fatty."

"Want to hear updates about our efforts to keep you

from hanging by your neck until dead?" I said.

"What I want is a girl. Bring me some ass."

I sighed, world-weary ronin that I was.

"Let's talk Juanita Yates."

He sagged a little. "The cleaning lady. Who cares about her."

"You did."

"Did not."

"Would it surprise you to learn Juanita Yates wasn't her real name?"

His eyebrows lifted and for the first time he looked directly at me.

He *was* surprised. I knew it. Mackenzie August, master sleuth.

"So," he said. "I don't care."

"Did you know she was intimate with her other clients?"

"Intimate."

"To use your phrase," I said. "Screwing."

"No she wasn't."

"How do you know?"

"I don't. I don't know, *fatty*. And I don't care."

"It would behoove you to admit you and Juanita were romantic," I said.

"We weren't...romantic. I was being kind to her. The stupid Mexican whore."

"Admit the dalliance to the prosecution and it might lessen your sentence," I said.

"Up yours, Matt."

"Mackenzie."

"Whatever, both of you. Nothing happened between us," he said, issuing spittle.

"Prove it."

"Prove what?"

"Prove there was nothing romantic between you two."

"How," he said.

"Provide me with your Facebook password."

He leaned backwards in his chair. Visibly surprised. "Why?"

"You two communicated that way, I'm guessing."

"No."

"No what?"

"No we *didn't*," he said.

"Prove it, with your password."

"No."

"This is a fun game. Why not?"

"Because," he said. "Because...that's how I communicate with all my friends. And they share *important* secrets that you can't see. Because you're *poor*."

"You idiot," I said. "You're paying me a fortune. Let me help you."

"Figure out another way, fatty."

"What the hell happened on that dock, Grady? Why'd you shoot her?"

"I killed her," he said and he looked as though proud of it. "I killed Juanita. That's her real name, I'm sure of it. I shot Juanita with the wild west gun. Because that's what guys like me and my friends do."

"You don't have any friends, Grady."

"Hah, shows what you know, *fatty*. Why else would I be in here?"

I was struck with a realization as I watched him gloat, sailing cleanly past logic and reason. It was a realization I should have reached earlier.

Grady Huff *liked* being in prison. The incarceration and the upcoming trial and its insinuations filled him with self-importance. He felt like he was someone to be reckoned with, perhaps for the first time in his life. He felt like the friends he didn't have were gossiping about him with overtones of approval.

"Oh crud," I said.

"What?"

"My client is an ignoramus so broken he doesn't even desire fixing."

He frowned. "What? Who's your client?"

"Never mind."

LATER THAT MORNING I parked in the Wells Fargo tower on the third deck and checked my phone.

Ronnie had texted.

>> **I am mortified. And I feel like death.**

>> **I remember very little from last night.**

>> **I was shocked to wake up in your guest bed, and you already gone.**

>> **Please don't hold it against me. We'll have another first date. It'll be perfect. And I will be a princess.**

I grinned and replied.

Don't feel bad. I had a good time. You were fun, including the upheaval.

Besides, I had to get you into bed. Which included removing your lovely red dress. And I witnessed your new lingerie.

I'm still glowing.

>> **You're sweet.**

>> **I'll make it up to you.**

>> **Twice.**

>> **One of these days.**

>> **Sigh.**

>> Talk soon. I'm racing for Va Beach.

Before getting out of the car I took a moment to luxuriate in the memory of her tiny lingerie. It had been a sight so powerful I already had nostalgia.

Lesser men would have cried.

Not Mackenzie August. I merely took the coldest shower of my life.

My basking over, I boarded the elevator to the fifteenth floor. A senior engineer named Joel Stevens met me at the doors of AECOM and gave me a brisk handshake. He had a gosh darn pocket protector, though otherwise Joel appeared to be a competent man in full. Decent head of brown hair, wireframe glasses, strong jaw.

We went to his office, which was more like a glorified cubicle. The carpet was a thin blue weave, and out his window I could see most of southern Roanoke, including Mill Mountain Star.

"Great view," I said. "Our city is darling."

"Star city of the south."

He played jazz on his Bose speaker and set his chair close to mine.

"I am dismayed," I said. "I don't see a drafting table or protractor. No blue prints. Aren't you an engineer?"

He grinned and nodded towards the three computer monitors. "I haven't used a drafting table since college. Everything is digital. Instead of a protractor I use AutoCAD and SAFE and Navisworks."

"Sometimes I feel like Rip Van Winkle," I said. "We're living in the future."

"Times change so fast, these state of the art programs are already out of date. So, Alvin Bradley called me and said I should meet with you."

"Alvin Bradley, the friendly neighborhood Miller salesman. Did he tell you why?"

"I have a guess," said Joel.

"Questions about Carlotta."

He nodded. Shifted uncomfortably. Reached to the Bose speaker and turned it up another notch, and scooted his chair closer to mine. "It is imperative this conversation be discreet."

"Understood. Nothing will leave the cubicle without your permission."

"I had an affair with Carlotta," said Joel.

"Wow, you don't beat around the bush."

"I'm a busy man. Beating around the bush is superfluous. And Alvin said I can trust you. I've known him for twenty years," he said.

"Carlotta is dead."

"You're kidding."

"Nuh uh."

"How about that," said Joel. He had the look of a man discovering he'd gotten the answer wrong on a complex math problem. "Alvin didn't tell me."

"Her killer confessed and he's in jail."

He tugged at his ear. "Sorry, you caught me by surprise. I'm a little speechless."

"I'm trying to figure out what happened. The killer will be in jail a long time, no matter what. But I suspect it wasn't an unprovoked homicide," I said.

"What is it you do for a living? Police detective?"

"Private."

"You're massive," he said. I received the impression he wanted to weigh and measure me.

"Very astute, Joel."

"I have a theory about Carlotta. I might be way off, but it's an educated guess."

"I'm all ears. My guesses are uneducated and ignorant."

"Perhaps the killer didn't want to be extorted," he said.

"Extorted," I repeated.

"Carlotta was extorting me. Two thousand dollars a month."

"Two thousand," I whistled. A clue! I loved those. "She threatened to reveal the affair?"

"Correct," said Joel. He was leaning towards me, our faces less than a foot apart, and talking in a hushed tone. "Carlotta cleaned my home for several months. She became sexually forthright. I complied. It went on a while and we both agreed it was purely recreational. Eventually I got engaged to another woman, my wife now, who wanted to wait until marriage for sex. She's sweet but she's a puritan. Carlotta told me she would never reveal the evidence of our tryst if I paid her two grand a month for one year."

"Could she prove the tryst?"

"She could. Unbeknownst to me, her brother filmed us skinny dipping. I don't know *what* I was thinking, very out of character for me. I lead a buttoned-up life. It was her idea. Anyway. I make decent money and didn't want to horrify my fiancée, who is now my wife, and I figured it was a good investment."

"Were Carlotta's sexual services the reason you recommended her to Alvin?"

"No. I didn't recommend her, per se. He came over once while she was there, saw her, and hired her on the spot. Carlotta is exceptionally pretty. Was pretty, I mean. And keep in mind, I wasn't married or engaged when the tryst began. I thought we were just having some innocent fun."

"Not so innocent."

"No. How long ago was she murdered?"

"Approximately nine months," I said.

"Damn. I wasted eighteen thousand. But I suppose her brothers might demand payment anyway."

"Her two brothers. I heard about them," I said.

"Nasty guys. Came here, to my *office*, the one time I was late on payment."

"Deals with the devil are not without consequence," I said.

"You bet. You'll get no self-pity from me. I reaped what I sowed. So we can keep all this between us?"

"Absolutely."

"Have I helped?" asked Joel.

"I'd like to meet these brothers."

"Yeah?"

"Would you consider ceasing the blackmail payments and calling me if they show their faces?" I said.

"It would be my pleasure, Mr. August."

Back in the parking lot I walked and I whistled.

I was learning things. Divining germane actualities.

Juanita/Carlotta's primary business wasn't cleaning houses, it was extortion. She carefully selected lonely and potentially stupid men, seduced them, and then began the bargaining process. You give me money and I'll shut up. If her clients wouldn't see reason, she'd call in her brothers. And possibly play the video tape.

She'd only started cleaning George's house, the guy at the lake with the tan who drank White Russians in the morning. She hadn't begun the seduction process with him yet, though he did think she had an ass like a butterball ham.

She'd seduced Alvin and gotten to the skinny dipping phase but then Sally caught them, ruining her bargaining power. Carlotta even called in the brothers, but to no effect because Sally had already thrown him out and Alvin had an army of big friends at the warehouse.

She'd seduced Joel and successfully extorted him.

She'd seduced Grady Huff and gotten shot.

I was closer to the truth but still hadn't arrived. Grady Huff would never shoot Juanita/Carlotta to avoid blackmail. One thing he had in spades was expendable income. If she had threatened to expose their sexual congress then I bet Grady would have made her an even better offer—let's keep screwing and I'll pay you a fortune. Because one thing he didn't have was affection and companionship. If Juanita/Carlotta had been after money then Grady was a gold mine.

He'd shot her for a different reason—not money. I was still walking in the dark but now possibly facing the right direction.

I still didn't know what happened on that dock.

But...did I need to? I only needed enough to make Darren Robbins and the prosecution flinch.

How did I do that? Grady refused to talk. The dummy liked jail. I had essentially promised Joel and Alvin that I wouldn't drag their dirty laundry into the light. They'd never consent to testimony on trial under oath.

Either way, Candice Hamilton would be pleased. And I liked it when she was pleased.

I neared my car.

A black sedan on my right roared to life. The lights

flared and tires squealed, loud in the enclosed parking deck. The sedan surged forward to squash me.

I jumped in time to prevent the front bumper from destroying my knees.I landed hard on the hood and rolled up the windshield.

As I flailed helplessly like an idiot, I realized I'd seen this black sedan before. It had followed me from Claytor Lake.

Darren Robbins's goons?

I hit the deck. Sometimes being tall and wide just meant it hurt when you fell over.

The black sedan clipped the rear bumper of a Porsche Boxster and stopped, fifteen feet away. I came up with my Kimber 1911 out of the clip at my side. Stayed in a kneeling position and took aim.

The black sedan's brake lights ignited. The passenger door opened and a man started to emerge. I thumbed off the safety and squeezed. The Kimber kicked and popped.

I missed—blasted the interior handle of the door instead.

The guy yelled something, ducked back inside and the sedan lurched forward again. I fired another round, punching a hole in the rear windshield. Ineffective.

The black sedan squealed around the corner, quickly retreating down the parking deck. It had no rear plates, removed for the express purpose of stymieing my vast intelligence.

I climbed to my feet. Considered chasing. But by the time I got my keys out, slid behind the wheel, fired up the Honda and got it pointed in the right direction, they'd be home free.

"Not cool, Darren Robbins," I said, examining the hole I'd ripped in my jeans.

25

Finally, at nine on Saturday night, I got Kix to sleep. Though he had nearly killed me via tantrum.

Dad! he screamed. *What the HECK are you doing? You know I HATE sleeping. We should PARTY! I'm SO mad.*

A little frazzled, I went to the fridge for a beer.

Timothy August was in the kitchen at the small breakfast nook table, sitting in the dark. Bifocals perched on his nose, scanning the news on his iPad.

"Your meeting is tonight?"

"Yes sir," I said, twisting the top off a Yuengling.

"And you'll come home from it?"

"I'm gonna try."

He leaned backwards in his chair and let out a breath through his nose. Took off the bifocals and squeezed the bridge of his nose with his thumb and forefinger. "You know I hate this."

"I know."

"This is hard for a father," he said.

"I'm sorry."

"You have to do it?"

I sat across from him and set the drink down. "I do. I think I'm paying the price for a lifetime of accumulating questionable decision-making. Joining the LAPD. Becoming a violent man. Working homicide. Letting the violence have some authority in my life a few years. Moving here and trying to clean up. Making the conscious decision to pursue justice and mercy, even if it cost me. Getting involved with Ronnie. Refusing to get uninvolved with Ronnie. Making myself a target. It kinda all adds up to tonight. A contest of wills with other men like me to determine who gets to stay and who has to go."

"The danger you're in is extreme."

"But it's even worse for Ronnie," I said.

"Why can't you tell Stackhouse where this meeting is? Let her go in with a SWAT team and arrest everyone."

"They'd kill her. If not tonight then very soon. And besides, I got myself into this mess," I said and I drained most of the Yuengling.

Cheap but delicious. Like me.

"Have you considered the option of taking Ronnie and Kix and starting a new life somewhere else?"

"Same answer. I got myself into this mess. And at some point, you have to answer the question—who am I? And if I run then I don't know," I said.

The silence of the house sounded more profound than usual, residing between our words.

"I don't want to raise Kix alone," he said.

"I know."

"He will need his father. His future is worth more than a temporary show of pride this evening."

"If I thought the odds were too heavily stacked against me, I wouldn't go. This is a calculated risk and I think it'll work," I said.

"I'm still nervous."

"Makes two of us."

~

I PARKED downtown in a lot open to the public on the weekends, near the poker room. A handful of romantic couples were wandering past on the sidewalk, heading to the live music and dancing near the market.

I checked my watch. Going dancing at *this* hour? It was nine-thirty, for heaven's sake.

I looked at the tower above, lights burning on the fifth floor. Inhaled a deep breath and shrugged inside my sports jacket, taking comfort in the pressure of the gun on my hip. Tonight the air felt warm.

A man stepped out of the shadows. Like he'd been waiting for me.

"Hola Big Mack."

"The heck are you doing here?" I asked.

"Going to the meeting," said Manny. He was in jeans and a brilliant white linen shirt, sleeves rolled up, looking like the handsomest man on earth. "With all the *jefes*. And you, lowly gun for hire."

"How'd you discover the time and location?"

"You try to hide it. But I am a sneaky bastard, muchacho."

"You can't go up there. You're a federal marshal. They'd crap a brick. These guys are organized crime."

"But I am corrupt as hell," he said. "You go, I go."

"I have to do this, Manny."

"Sí, lo sé. And I have to go too. We amigos. You know what I am without you? Not a lot."

He stuck out his hand.

We shook. I hoped I wouldn't regret it.

"Okay. If you insist."

"Let's go get shot in the ass, señor."

We climbed the concrete stairwell to the fifth floor of the tower.

A guy named Freddie stopped us at the stairwell. He looked like a professional bodybuilder wearing a green suit. He had a tattoo of a dragon on his face. On his FACE. His head was shaved.

"Mack," he said. "One gun only. House rules."

"That's all I need," I said.

He stared at me blankly.

"Did I sound like Clint Eastwood? Cause I tried," I said.

He did not smile. Nor did the dragon tattoo on his face.

He patted me down.

"Cell phone stays in a basket outside the room," said Freddie. He voice was scratchy, as if someone had hit him in the throat. A lot.

"That's new."

Freddie shrugged, bunching his trapezoid muscles up to his ears. "Gotta be careful."

I acquiesced, dropping my iPhone into a basket full of other phones.

Freddie turned his eyes to Manny.

"You too, marshal."

Manny said, "*Simon*, huge honky. But maybe you tell Marcus I'm here. I do not think I am on the guest list."

"Manny the spic," said Freddie. More of a rasp. "The marshal. You're expected."

Manny grinned.

"Good to be wanted. I like your dragon."

Manny placed his phone in the basket and submitted to

inspection. Freddie let him keep his .357 but apprehended the ankle revolver.

The fifth floor was unfinished construction. Down a long hallway, several high stakes poker games were running. Music and laughter drifted our way, the games hidden from view by exposed 2x4s and heavy vinyl drapes and sporadic drywall.

Freddie led us to a room I'd previously visited twice. It was the size of a small apartment with the walls removed, dominated by a plush poker table and chairs. The floors were exposed subfloor, except for the rugs. Several lamps were set up. Drinks could be had from a small bar.

The men stood when we entered.

Manny and I were the last to arrive. Already at the table...

Edgar, owner of the building and also proprietor of several gun stores. A sharp black man, he dressed in black suits and his hair had fancy zigzag designs. He ran illegal firearms up and down the east coast. I'd also heard the rumor he strong-armed votes in the recent congressional election.

Clay Fleming, country gentleman dressed in cowboy boots and hat. He manufactured and sold illegal moonshine, and moved all manner of paraphernalia up and down the interstate.

Dexter, the shooter and shadow Darren Robbins brought with him.

Darren Robbins, pimp, prosecutor, prick.

Toby Moreno, professional hitman, swollen face, great hair.

Big Will, Marcus's right-hand man, a boss in the cocaine trade. Big biceps, red hoodie, bored expression.

And Marcus Morgan. Dressed in black and silver.

Marcus indicated we take the two seats to his left.

"Game's about to start," he said in that rich growl.

"Marcus," said Darren Robbins pointing at Manny. He kept his hand low, like shooting from the hip. "I know him, that's the federal marshal. Get him out of here."

"I invited Manny," said Marcus.

"I don't care, he's not part of this."

"Yeah. He is. My party, my rules."

"Marcus, listen to yourself," said Darren. "He's a cop. You're breaking the commandments. This is an official Kings convening."

"You guys have commandments? Are they written on stone?" I asked. "If I look directly at them, will I glow?"

Marcus indicated us with a tilt of his head. "Manny, this is your call. Your boy August, he requested this meeting. He's in it deep. You stay and you're in deep too. I can't and won't protect either of you, depending on what we decide. Other words, you can walk away. If you stay for the convening? Maybe you can't."

"I'll stay, señor. Looks to me like a fun crowd. We play pinochle?"

"Jesus Christ," said Darren and he looked to Toby for support. "This is amateur hour."

Toby agreed. "What'd I tell you."

Marcus addressed the men at the table. "Manuel Martinez, he's a cop but the man don't play the do-gooder game. He's done favors for us. He let Big Will's brother go. I owe him. What happens here, stays here, he knows."

Clay Fleming tilted his cowboys hat back a bit and said, "Good by me. More the merrier."

"No," said Darren. "More the merrier? Hell no. This isn't camp. This isn't a recreational t-ball team. We have rules for a reason. We don't let police into the inner circle and we don't let their friends in either. Both these junior varsity jokers, they'll be loose ends. And Marcus, the Kings will hear about the breaking of commandments."

"My word is good, Señor Robbins. Better than yours, I bet, eh?" said Manny and he grinned. "Maybe you shut up."

Darren scanned the room, outraged, the way I bet kindergarten teachers often did.

Marcus said, "Like it or not, he's part of this."

"A mistake," said Darren. "A lazy mistake. Might cost you."

Marcus stood as stoic and cool as usual. But I detected some heat under the veneer. "Who's gonna make me pay for this mistake? You? Could try. Not sure what good a law degree do you."

"This is official Kings business, Marcus. The *Kings*. We don't screw around with Omertà."

Omertà, I knew, was an ancient code of silence.

"Yo August," said Big Will, who had sat back down and appeared on the verge of sleep. "What'choo call it guys flex on each other? Sword fighting?"

"Saber rattling."

"That's right. Maybe we quit the saber rattling and play cards."

Dexter, Darren's shooter, casually set his gun on the table.

Darren Robbins addressed Manny. "Inspector August is a dead man, marshal. You can't stop it. You stay to play cards, you probably are too."

"I stay. Like in blackjack. You get it, *pendejo*?"

Darren shook his head and fiddled with the fat golden ring on his right hand. Looked like a college signet, maybe law school.

Big Will snickered.

During the pregnant pause, Carlos walked in. He wasn't as big or muscular as Freddie (no one was), but his t-shirt was tighter and his head equally shaved. He took his place behind Marcus and quietly crossed his arms.

Edgar, silent up till now, nodded slowly at Dexter and his firearm. "Get yo damn gun off my felt. I got rules too."

Dexter, without taking his eyes off Manny and me, replaced it inside his shoulder holster. "Bonnie and Clyde, you know how to play?"

I said, "We prefer Thelma and Louise. And we play a little."

"I look around this table," said Darren. "And I don't see one real card player. Nothing but rookies here."

Some of the ice in the room was breaking. Tensions lessened a little. We took our seats.

Edgar placed two decks of cards on the table.

We threw money at him and he slid stacks of colorful chips our way. Minimum $500. Maximum $1000. Mere change to these crime lords but they didn't play for monetary purposes. Twas all pride.

I threw in $500. And gulped.

Manny tossed in a big wad of twenties and received $1000 in chips.

Don't ask, don't tell.

"Carlos, my man," said Darren Robbins. "Get the music. I could do with some Sinatra."

Carlos went to the Bose speaker system and soon Frank was crooning.

Moreno stood to get himself a drink. Got one for Darren too, both drinking straight scotch.

Without being asked, Carlos brought me and Manny a couple Old Fashioned drinks.

Big Will drew the first deal. All the sounds were magnified. The pitter-patter and hiss of the shuffle. The clacking of chips. Clinking of ice.

Fly me to the moon.

"How's the chicanery business?" I asked Clay Fleming, the Floyd cowboy. "People still drink alcohol?"

"Yeah buddy, but you know what's a stick in my craw? Uncle Sam loosening the regulations on liquor. Moonshine is less exotic. Moving less jars these days."

"Fewer."

"What?"

"You're moving fewer jars," I said. "These things are important."

Clay grinned and shook his head.

"I found me a new racket. Moving cigarettes."

"That so," I said.

"Know how much a pack costs in New York City? Fifteen bucks. I gettem here for under five. I fill a bus with a thousand cartons and sell'em in a day. Ten packs to a carton. I clear fifteen thousand per trip. I can't move them bastards fast enough."

"Good man. Making us wealthy," said Darren.

"God bless nicotine," said Toby and he raised his glass to Clay.

We played several Texas Hold'em hands in silence.

We were each dealt two cards, and five cards were placed on the table with rounds of betting between. A player could bet any amount he wished.

Toby bet just like he punched—aggressive. So aggressively that Marcus trapped and busted him on the third hand. Five hundred dollars gone in under ten minutes. He grumbled about luck and bought five hundred more in chips.

After twenty minutes, Marcus said, "Much as I'd like to

play cards without business, that isn't why we convened. We here to talk Calvin Summers's stake in the business. And we here to talk about his daughter."

Darren stood and removed his sports jacket. He draped it carefully around the back of his chair. Rolled the sleeves of his shirt up, and undid the top couple buttons at the neck. "And," he said. "Don't forget our guest of honor, the gumshoe for hire. We'll determine how best to execute the son of a bitch."

"August, you called for this," said Marcus.

Edgar began dealing the next hand. Fip, fip, fip went the cards and they skidded across the felt.

"Why don't you begin."

I nodded at Marcus. Closed my eyes and tilted my head back a little. "Marcus Morgan, I want to thank you for helping me organize this meeting here today." I shrugged and held up my hands. Talked in a raspy voice. "How did things ever get so far? I don't know. It was so unfortunate. So unnecessary. Tattaglia lost a son. I lost a son. We're quits."

Toby made a snorting noise.

"Bastard's quoting *The Godfather*," he said.

"He what?" said Edgar.

"That's the Godfather, the big scene with Marlon Brando," said Toby. "Guy thinks he's funny."

"August," said Marcus. "Maybe don't be an ass."

"Just so everyone is up to speed," I said, dropping the impeccable impression of Vito Corleone. "Last week, Veronica Summers dumped Darren's sorry ass."

Dexter tensed. In my periphery, I thought Big Will did too.

Darren smiled to himself, looking at his cards. He played it cool but reddened.

I said, "She's renounced her role as prostitute for your

goon squad. I'm here to negotiate her complete release from your farcical claim to her."

"Lies," said Toby. "You got no proof. She don't want out."

Marcus leaned forward. Maybe only one degree, but it felt significant. "Veronica told me she's out. And you know it. You come here talking about the commandments? We speak only truth to each other, that's a commandment. So either you talk honestly or you keep your got'damn mouth shut."

To my surprise, Toby looked a little abashed.

I didn't understand the hierarchy of the Kings yet, but Marcus was no underling.

"Negotiate," said Edgar. "You said negotiate for her release. Explain."

"Darren claims Ronnie belongs to him. He says she'll either keep sleeping with whomever he decides or he'll kill her."

Darren spread his hands to the table, like appealing to reason. "One does not simply revoke his or her status in the underworld. Veronica Summers cannot walk away on a whim. Not even if there's a wannabe tough guy, a do-gooder private inspector filling her head with visions of roses and a bogus innocent life."

"You demand some sort of yubitsume ceremony?" I asked.

"You bit what?" said Clay Fleming, pulling a handful of chips his way, won with a pair of queens.

"Yubitsume," explained Darren. "A ritual of the Japanese Yakuza. You want out of the Japanese underworld, you chop off a finger. That's the penalty. It marks you. And no, Veronica doesn't leave so easily."

"Easily?" said Manny. "Ay dios mio."

Edgar said again, "Negotiate. August, what you got to negotiate with?"

I pointed at Dexter. Then at Darren. Then Toby.

"These three ass clowns beat the hell out of Ronnie. Three men, one woman. She had to drag herself to urgent care. And now they're threatening to coerce her return to prostitution. So I'm going to kill them."

Edgar's eyebrows rose above the level of his sunglasses.

Clay made a whistling sound.

I heard Carlos shift his weight behind me. The subfloor creaked.

"Maybe two of them," said Manny. He raised his hand like a kid in a classroom. "Me? I call dibs on at least one."

Marcus released a soft sigh. He knew.

He knew Manny and I had crossed into territory we wouldn't come back from. A place where he couldn't protect us.

I said, "You three gentlemen back off Ronnie, I'll let you live. That's the deal."

"Tell me, August," said Darren Robbins. He and I were playing a hand, only the two of us remained in. He slid in a big bet, maybe two hundred dollars. "What kind of man are you?"

I glanced at my cards. I was weak.

"I'm a man who doesn't bluff," I said. I folded—tossed in my cards and let him win the pot. "But I also don't lose."

Darren turned over his two cards—he had nothing. He'd been bluffing.

"You don't belong at this table. I'm a man who gets what he wants." He pulled the winnings his way and began stacking chips. "You see this? This is your money, inspector. A shame, you have precious little to begin with. But I will take it all."

"Does that mean you surrender?" I said.

"That means, no deal, rookie. You threatened me in front

of the gathering. Your fate is sealed. You should've been aced last week but Marcus cashed in some credit. Two diamonds' worth. God knows why."

"One of us is gonna die, huh," I said.

"One of us."

"Mercutio's soul is but a little ways above our heads," I said, quoting my favorite play from high school. "And either thou or I or both must go with him."

Toby frowned. His face was still swollen and the motion caused his left eye to close. "The hell does that mean?"

"Thou wretched boy," said Darren, completing the line. "Shall with him hence."

"How about that? You can read," I said. "I assumed you still looked at picture books."

There was a lull. We played several more hands. No one spoke, like the first round of a fight had ended and we were getting our breath. Marcus won a big pot off Big Will. Toby took one off Dexter.

Marcus said, "So you two assholes gonna kill each other. That's squared. Now we talk about Calvin and his assets."

Clay Fleming said, "Calvin's pot still growing? What's-his-name still tending the fields?"

"Rueben, and yes. Acres of the shit," said Marcus. "Represents millions. And it belongs to Ronnie Summers. Time being, let's focus on that. She inherited a variety of investments, but we only worried about the fields of hash."

"Isn't one of the things she inherited," I asked, "a seat at this table?"

Marcus and Darren glanced at one another.

"More or less," said Marcus.

I said, "How great for Ronnie, her possessions being parsed in absentia, so her feeble mental powers won't be taxed."

"This is a table for grownups," said Darren. "For men. Veronica Summers is a toy. She's a toy I dangle in front of colleagues to keep them loyal, to keep them horny. She doesn't get to sit here."

Darren and I were in another hand together. I'd just taken a fair amount off Dexter, who fumed. It put me around $700.

"Enlighten me. Why not?" I asked. I had a pair of 10s and I made a modest bet.

Darren immediately raised me. Something like $360. "Because I said so."

"Ah. The airtight reasoning of bad elementary teachers," I said.

"She's an *item*. A thing to be used. Everyone at this table has had her. Or did you not know that? You didn't, did you. How sad. You think she loves you? She's a professional slut. And she doesn't. Get to. Sit here," said Darren.

I did *not* know everyone at the table had had her.

I took a moment to collect myself.

"Your ears are turning purple, gumshoe," said Darren. "That a tell? Or are you about to cry?"

I showed him my cards. A pair of 10s.

"I fold," I said. Folding meant surrender. He won.

He exposed his cards. He had nothing. Another bluff. I could have won if I hadn't folded.

"I don't need to ask again. But I will. What kind of man are you?" he said. "I'll tell you. It's obvious. You're a weak man. Scared. You don't have what it takes."

I stayed quiet.

I had a plan. I hoped it would work. Eventually.

But so far this was harder than I anticipated.

Mackenzie August, swimming up stream.

Marcus said, "Maybe Veronica, she should be at the next meeting. But that ain't what we're discussing tonight."

"Listen. Marcus, about Calvin's marijuana. You're making this harder than it has to be," said Darren. He was shuffling the deck.

Big Will and Edgar and Clay, they were all staying quiet. Letting the more powerful players reckon things.

He said, "This is how it'll go, Marcus. With your approval. The gumshoe is dead. His boy Manny too. That isn't up for debate. I'll give Veronica one last chance. She either returns to Washington to play ball, so to speak, or she's aced. Either way, we take the marijuana. She doesn't get a say-so."

"She owns the fields," said Marcus. "That's something we honor. She's a stakeholder."

"Only through inheritance. I respect the commandments. But I'll find a way. The Kings will approve," said Darren.

"So you'll take what you want," I said.

"That's right, gumshoe. You're catching on. A little too late, though."

"Know what I can't figure out," I said. "Why you get a seat at the table."

He chuckled. Silly Mackenzie.

"See," I said. "Ronnie's been kicked around her whole life. She fought through it. Paid her way. Mother died, got no help from her father. Abused by old men. Abused by you. And yet, here she is—growing as a person. Getting stronger. Smarter. Changing her mind about important things. Earning her way to the top. She's taken your punishment and come out the other side. Whereas you? You were born rich. Your old man gave you everything. You only got into

Michigan Law because your father bought you in—I checked. Privilege made you soft. And being wealthy still isn't enough. You're the fat kid at lunch getting fatter. And you don't deserve to be at any table with Veronica Summers."

There was a hush. Like a storm had just passed, leaving the world in silence.

Big Will laughed quietly through his nose.

The next hand was dealt. I had an A-2 of spades.

I bet $50. Darren called. Everyone else folded. They knew this hand was important.

The first three cards flopped. A-2-8.

I had two pair. As and 2s. Strong. But the 2 and 8 were hearts. If another heart came, I could lose to a flush.

I bet $100.

Darren matched it.

"The fat kid getting fatter," he said.

"That's right. You're not going to win. Not this poker game. Not the trial with Grady Huff. And not against Ronnie," I said.

Big Will was dealing.

He placed down the fourth card.

It was a ten of clubs. No harm but no help.

I checked, which was a sign of surrender.

Darren grinned. He pushed in $260.

I thought about it.

"Wrong on all accounts," said Darren. "I'll beat you at this poker game, you piece of shit. You have no chance of getting Grady a lesser sentence. And I'll rape Veronica Summers in front of you."

"Sure you won't change your mind?" I said. "To me, that's a sign of maturity. Ronnie's mature. You're just the fat kid stealing cookies."

"August. You're an amateur. It's a waste of my time talking to you."

I slid the $260 into the pot. Darren blinked twice and sat up straighter.

My hand didn't shake. But it was close.

Dear Lord, don't let there be another heart.

Edgar dealt the final card.

It was a heart. Three hearts on the table, making a flush possible.

But it was the ace of hearts. I had a full house. AAA22. Unbeatable.

"You may win this poker game," I said. "But you can't beat Ronnie. She's better than you. Stronger. Smarter."

"Focus on the game, rookie. You lost this hand and you know it," said Darren. "I dare you to bluff. Go ahead, push money in."

I didn't bet.

I said, "Check."

He took my action as surrender.

"That's what I thought. You aren't a man. You're like Veronica. I take what I want out of your ass. And you can't even resist. I'm all-in," he said.

He had just bet all his money.

He and I held eye contact. He absently fiddled with the ring.

"You're out of your league," I said. He frowned. He glanced at the cards and then back at me. "Especially with Ronnie."

"Fold your cards, gumshoe. You're done."

"You're out of your league," I said again. "Even with Grady Huff. He's not getting first degree."

"Christ, the mouth on you. Shut up and act."

I slid all my money in. "I call."

"Hah," he cried. A loud sound that caused Clay to jump. Darren showed his cards. "You got played for a fool. I have the nut flush. To the king. You're a joke, August."

"Yikes," I said.

"You're broke. Go home."

"You have the flush," I said.

"That's right." Darren reached for the chips. "Thanks for playing."

"That's a good hand."

Something in my voice made him pause. He glanced at the cards on the table again. "That's right..."

"Almost as good as my full house."

"Bull shit," he said.

"You're taking the wrong cookies, rich kid," I said.

I showed him.

Three aces and a pair of 2s.

"Aces full," I said. "Get your hands off my damn money, Robbins."

Big Will threw his hands up and laughed.

Clay whistled and clapped a few times.

Marcus Morgan grinned.

Darren was too stunned to move.

It was at that moment that Veronica Summers walked into the room.

26

The game froze.

Hip cocked, Ronnie paused in the doorway, allowing us a long inspection. She wore black heels (strappy Jimmy Choos, unless I missed my guess), a Harley black leather mini skirt, and a slim-fitting white button-up. Collar flicked wide, buttons undone down to her solar plexus, providing a tease of the dainty red lingerie underneath.

Had an albino Bengal tiger wandered in, we might've been less astounded. Or had Christie Brinkley, or Cindy Crawford, Heidi Klum, or who ever it was the boys gawked at these days. Compared to the pack of us ugly idiots, she was so gorgeous it hurt my eyes.

"Hello gentlemen," she said and she strode in, heels clicking. "You started without me."

No one responded. Like we'd been caught doing something naughty and we awaited our fate. I had no reason to feel guilty but I did.

She must've been outside the last few days—her cheeks and nose had a pinkish healthy suntan. Her blonde hair was held back by a pair of sunglasses. The facial contusions had entirely healed except for a little scarring at the outside corner of her right eye. That might be permanent.

I started to rise but she said, “Don’t get up, handsome.”

Not sure if that bought me street cred with the fellas or not.

She stopped at the head of the table between Clay and me. We scooted our chairs, making room for her. She set her crimson purse on the poker table. Edgar looked like he wanted to object but didn’t.

Ronnie winked at Fleming. “Get me a drink, would you, Clay? Something that’s gin forward.”

Clay leapt to obey.

Fat Susie came in, followed by Freddie. Freddie was grinning happily, which caused the facial dragon to ripple.

Ronnie bent her right leg at the knee, kept her left straight. Leaned forward over the table and placed her fingertips on the felt. At the moment, those were the longest legs in the world.

The gentlemen at the table didn’t know whether to crane our necks to look at her legs, keep our eyes on her face, or let them wander down her open shirt.

We were a mess. It was the sudden shock of so much skin.

“I need to catch up,” she said. “What have I missed?”

For a moment, she received no reply.

“Clearly you need a stenographer,” she said. “Cat got your tongue, boys?”

Darren cleared his throat. “How did you—“

“I wasn’t talking to you, my dear,” she said. “Someone else, please.”

Darren’s eyes bulged.

Manny, normally unflappable, raised his hand. He

looked a little cowed. Her total control of the room was that strong.

"Yes Manny."

"So far we have decided that Mack will kill Darren and his stupid amigos because they threatened you. And then Darren will kill Mack. And also me. Also Darren will rape you and maybe kill you. And that maybe Darren is bad at cards."

"Thank you, Manny."

"De nada, senorita."

"Distressing news. What did we decide about my father's fields of marijuana?"

"That Darren, he will steal the fields even if he let you live," said Manny. "He figure out a loophole to seize them."

Darren shifted in his chair. Somehow, some way, everything was going against him and he didn't know how to stop it. He said, "That's not exactly—"

Ronnie turned her bright eyes onto Marcus. "Marcus, I'm surprised. I expected better from you."

Marcus squirmed.

How the hell was Ronnie doing this? Why was she in charge?

I knew how. She'd caught us by surprise and now she pressed her advantage. The better question was, would anyone dare stand up to her?

Marcus said, "That course of action, Darren proposed it. I would never sign off."

"Oh real nice, Marcus," said Darren.

Clay returned with Ronnie's drink. Something clear and swirly with a coil of orange peel. She sat in Clay's chair and accepted the drink without comment.

Clay, the poor guy, didn't know what to do so he stood beside Carlos, behind me.

"And the rest of you? You approve of Darren's plan?" she said.

She reached down to fiddle with her shoes, little scooping motions. Then she raised her feet, set her bare legs on the poker table, crossed at the ankles. Edgar looked pained.

Her toenails matched the red lingerie.

"I do not approve of Darren's plan," I said.

"Why not?" she asked.

"I prefer you alive. Which is true of myself too. And besides, I am besotted with you."

Toby made a weird choking sound.

"So? They are too," she said, indicating the silent host with the hand that held her drink.

"But I am fonder of you than I am of myself or of money," I said. "Which gives me some freedom to stand up for what I believe."

She nodded simply.

Toby thought about getting to his feet but changed his mind, caught halfway between. He looked around for support. "So...who cares if she's here? We still have business to discuss...right?"

Ronnie turned her eyes on him. Her calves, resting on the table, rubbed together a little.

"Or...maybe..." said Toby and he lost his steam. "I don't know."

I read somewhere that men became stupider in the presence of beautiful women. They perform poorly on tests, that kind of thing. Their cognitive resources become invested in the woman and they can't do other things well anymore.

Watching the men at the table, I concurred with theory.

"So Mackenzie is to be murdered and I am to be raped," she said and she sipped her drink. "And my property to be taken. Homicide, sexual assault, and grand larceny in the first degree. Yes?"

"That's the idea," said Big Will in his high-pitched voice that sounded like Mike Tyson's, "offered by the honkies up north."

"I know the code. I know the commandments. What gives you the right?" she asked.

"August's earned his fate a dozen times over," said Darren.

I shrugged and took a sip of my Old Fashioned.

"Potentially true. I struggle with impulse control."

Clay guffawed.

"And me?" asked Ronnie.

Toby said, "Maybe you don't walk away from your job with Darren and you don't worry about that."

Ronnie did the thing again where she repositioned her legs. The muscles pressed and slid together, and her tiny skirt slid half an inch farther up. Toby fell quiet.

As a child I'd seen the televised and censored version of *Basic Instinct*, unbeknownst to my parents. There was a scene where Sharon Stone used her beauty and her raspy voice and her legs to render a group of professional detectives into a pack of blithering idiots.

Something like that was happening here. She was utilizing her body like a precision instrument. Not even I, bastion of nobility and etiquette, was impervious.

I've since been told that I missed some of the finer points in that Sharon Stone scene.

Darren said, "Keep your end of the bargain, Summers. We had a deal."

She made a tsk'ing sound.

"A deal in which my choices are to be prostituted or raped?"

"If the shoe fits..."

"I have a new deal for you," she said. She took another drink and set the glass down. "Everyone ready to listen?"

Marcus leaned backward in his chair. "I think we're all ears."

"I've had sex with most of you," she said. "Or at least, something to that effect. Either my father or Darren demanded it and you didn't object. Edgar. Dexter. Darren. Toby. Big Will. Clay. Freddie."

The names caused a latent grief somewhere inside me.

Everyone did the math. Who got left out?

Carlos, Marcus, Manny, and me.

She continued, "I was also blackmailed and forced into sex with most of Darren's powerful buddies in Washington. And so, I've seen too much. I know too many secrets. But I'm no longer under your control. I'm a loose end which needs to be tied off. Right?" she said.

Marcus nodded. "Something like that."

She held out her hand. "Reginald, my bag please."

Fat Susie walked forward and set a satchel in her grasp. In Fat Susie's other hand, a pistol. The man expected trouble.

"I propose a peace offering. And to show you I mean business..." she said and she reached into her satchel.

I tensed.

We all tensed.

She set an oblong sex toy on the poker table.

Good grief.

Everyone relaxed. Everyone except Darren.

"That vibrating gadget does not belong to me," she said. "It belongs to counselor Darren Robbins."

"Veronica..." he said. An edge of panic.

"During sex he uses it. But he does not apply it to his partner."

I looked at the gadget and then at Darren.

We all looked at the gadget and then at Darren.

"...Oooooh," I said. The implications were a little raunchy.

Big Will jumped up from his chair, covered his mouth, and released a high-pitched cackle.

"Weird ass honky!"

"A lie," said Darren, a deep shade of purple. "The bitch is lying."

Ronnie reached into her bag and produced a thin manila envelope with the word 'Darren' written in permanent marker. The envelope was sealed by bendable clasps. She tossed it onto the table.

"Don't believe me?" she said. "There's photographic evidence."

"She's bluffing," scoffed Toby and he reached for the envelope.

"Touch that and I'll take your hand off," said Darren in a low cold voice. "Anyone touches that, I'll kill the man."

"Freaky freaky stuff," said Big Will, still grinning.

Ronnie began tossing more envelopes onto the table. Labeled Dexter, Toby, Clay, and Freddie. Five total.

"And there's more," she said. "Of all the old guys in Washington."

I had a flashback. Of a conversation with Ronnie where she told me she had the ability to blackmail her abusers.

But I'd forgotten. Now here she was, bravely forcing her way through the crucible.

I said helpfully, "Should someone look inside? Someone should probably look."

"No," said Darren and Toby simultaneously.

Ronnie, legs still on the table, patted her red purse. "See the buckle? It's a camera and microphone. I started recording about a year ago, for the purposes of self-preservation. I got the idea from a Stieg Larsson book. Don't fret, I unplugged it for this meeting. No one needs to see this."

Dexter mumbled something under his breath.

Ronnie said, "Inside each envelope are photographs and transcripts of the audio. Guys, you might want to take my word for it—they are highly embarrassing."

Manny raised his hand again. "Señorita, there is no folder for Big Will."

Ronnie smiled. It was truly a lovely sight. "That's because Big Will is a perfect gentleman. He hides it, but Big Will is a romantic at heart. I have no desire to blackmail him."

Manny said, "And Edgar? No pictures?"

Edgar released a long sigh and leaned backwards in his chair.

Ronnie said, "Despite my best efforts, Edgar refused to cooperate. He accepted my father's offer for the sake of appearance only. I have nothing to blackmail him with. Edgar is gay."

"Didn't know that," said Marcus. He said it as if talking about tomorrow's weather.

Dexter spoke between clenched teeth. "No folder for the got'damn bullshit gumshoe?"

"Mackenzie?" said Ronnie. "That's because, although I undress and throw myself at him at frequent intervals, he hasn't assented. Yet. Also, I would not blackmail Mackenzie. Because if I'm being honest with myself and with you, I am head over heels in love with him. To such an extent somedays it's hard to breathe."

I felt like someone electrocuted me.

Manny made a loud hooting sound and clapped me on the back.

"You two!" he said. "I am the happiest spic. He won't say it but he loves you too, Miss Ronnie."

"I sincerely hope so." A deeper patina highlighted her cheeks.

I wanted to reply but couldn't.

"Ain't this cute," said Dexter, teeth still clenched. "Fucking cute. You just got yourself killed, bitch."

"Easy, Dex. We need to be smart," said Darren.

"At some point you'll need to examine the evidence of the envelopes," she said. "Trust me, it's worse than you fear. Copies of each envelope, and all the others I have, are in the hands of two local reporters. In the event of my death, they are instructed to open the envelopes and report on their contents. There is also a box ready to mail to a larger news outlet in Washington. You will each be humiliated and ruined."

Darren nodded. Sweat beaded at his hairline. "Understood. Nicely done, Veronica."

"I'm not finished," she said. "I'm overhauling the Kings's prostitution racket. It's deplorable and disgusting and it will not continue in its current form. Resist me and every one of us is going to jail."

Toby held up his hands, appealing to reason. "Be serious, Summers. It's the world's oldest profession. There's lonely stupid assholes on every block. Whoring is a gold mine. You just get rid of it?"

"Of course not. I'm not ignorant enough to try, Toby. I'm improving it so the girls are treated and paid better. I can't solve all the problems in the world, but I can dramatically improve this part of it. It'll become a voluntary profession, not forced servitude."

Marcus said, "You tackling a big problem, Veronica. Goes all the way up to the board, the Kings themselves."

"I've had half the Kings in bed and I have evidence. They'll play ball."

"Okay, Veronica, okay," said Darren. "We can figure this out."

"There's nothing to figure out. I've accepted that I need to pay for my sins. And I am. I'm prepared to die. The question is, are you?"

"Yeah," said Dexter. "I am."

"Well I'm not," said Darren Robbins. "So go easy, Dex."

"You boys and your hormones," said Ronnie. "Your dicks make you so stupid. You quickly need to realize—I have you by the balls; I own you."

A somber heaviness settled around the shoulders of the room. She was right. They were caught, pants down.

I decided to lighten the mood by stacking the $1,500 in front of me. The clacking chips sounded mellifluous to my ears, and I assumed to all the rest.

Should I whistle a jocose melody? I might.

Dexter sniffed. "This is bullshit. Let's ace the bitch, right?"

"You heard her," said Darren. He tilted his head back to finish his drink, ice tinkling. Wiped his mouth. "She's got the evidence to put us away."

"Not if she's dead."

"The reporters, Dex. Don't be a stupid rookie. I believe her."

"It's a bluff."

"No. It's not. Shut your got'damn mouth," said Darren. "That's all you know how to do, get your gun off. Cooler heads need to prevail. Let someone with a college degree do the thinking, got it?"

Dexter went quiet. I could see the gears turning behind his eyes—he wasn't handling the paradigm shift well. The sudden diplomacy had thrown him, and now the slut ran things? That made no sense. He grew still and even more quiet. An inner absence.

I saw it coming. So did Manny.

Dexter went for his pistol. Kill the bitch and figure the rest out later.

He was quick.

I surged forward, like a bull lunging. The chips and cards popped up as confetti. The felt table steamrolled into the lap of Dexter, Darren and Toby.

I blanked out. Even in retrospect I have no memory of the event.

For a long moment my vision was full of three guys from Washington taking turns hitting Ronnie in an alley. And her taking the punishment and refusing to back down. And me not being there to help.

Pent up anger released. Every muscle in my body flexed and clenched and bunched, and I ground my teeth so hard I'm surprised they didn't break.

Dunno if it was a hallucination or an out of body experience or what. But for an undetermined period of time, my mind shut me out.

I came to as Marcus was firmly pulling me backwards.

"It's over, August. It's over, babe, you hear me? Ease up. Let go, Mack," he said. Like speaking underwater.

My vision cleared. My chest heaved.

The world refocused.

Dexter was dead. I knew because I had his neck in my hands.

His throat looked like pulpy ribbons between my fists. His esophagus was punctured, broken by my thumbs. I'd pulled him apart. His exposed arteries still pumped weakly and blood spilled everywhere. His eyes bulged. From the knees down he was trapped under the poker table, me kneeling on his stomach.

I had choked him and squeezed and I'd been unable to stop.

I attempted reconnecting with my fingers but it took a concerted effort for them to cooperate. They released Dexter and I raised up.

Sounds and awareness rushed back in.

Everyone was on their feet.

Darren and Toby had their pistols out, aimed at me. Carlos had planted himself as a shield between us. He clenched his eyes, prepared to soak up gunfire.

Manny (a .357) and Ronnie (a little .380) and Fat Susie (Glock 17) each had a pistol out, held over Carlos's shoulders, aiming at Darren and Toby.

"It's over," Marcus said again. "Right? Be cool."

"Right," I said. The word emerged like a groan.

"Good hell, it ain't over," Toby barked. "The lunatic killed Dexter."

"Look at the poor bastard," said Darren. "Look at his throat. It's gone. I didn't know that was possible."

"Me either," said Manny. But he looked happy about it.

Edgar was so bereft he took off his sunglasses. "Damn it, my floors. Freddie, find some towels. The closet, maybe. Table's ruined too. The hell's the matter w'you. Supposed to be men of honor."

"And women," said Manny.

"Put your guns down," Marcus ordered. "Now. There's no violence at an official convening."

"Marcus, examine your loafers," said Darren. "The leather is covered with Dex. No violence my ass."

"Dexter broke the rules. Went for his piece. Paid the price. It's done."

Freddie came back. Threw a couple towels on the broken poker table. Pressed a roll of paper towels into my hands and backed away.

"Veronica, you go first," said Marcus. He stood between the two opposing groups, arms raised, palms out. Not directly in the line of fire, like Carlos. "Put your gun down first, babe. We get out of here alive."

"If you insist." Her voice sounded jarring and beautiful, a contradistinction against the carnage. She pulled her little .380 away. I heard the click of a safety. The gun went into her purse.

Next, Darren lowered his.

I looked at my red fingernails and grimaced. My stomach heaved.

"Reginald," said Ronnie. "This has been charming but I need to return to Street Ransom. Help the girls get settled. Coming?"

"Yes ma'am," he said and he holstered his Glock.

That left only Toby and Manny with guns out. Toby was glaring. I couldn't see Manny but I bet he was grinning. And possibly winking at his foil.

Ronnie stepped into her heels. "Good night, gentlemen. Our deal is firmly in place. I'll be in touch." She caught my eye. "Sooner or later, according to your merit and sex appeal."

She left. Fat Susie rumbled after.

On the ground Dexter's corpse released a bubbling sigh from the ruined larynx.

"Got'damn," said Toby. "That bitch worth all this?"

"Yeah," I said. "She is."

27

The following morning at breakfast, Kix and I appeared dressed in our Sunday best—both of us in loafers, khakis, and shirt and tie. Neither of us wore socks because we aren't animals.

Timothy August put down his mug of coffee. Sheriff Stackhouse smiled and waved lazily from her spot on the couch. She wore the indecent nightgown that I refused to inspect closely.

Timothy said, "Nice to see you, son."

"You too, Pops."

"I didn't fall asleep until you and Manuel came home."

"You ratted me out," I said. Withering him with scorn. "To Manny."

"I did. Was there violence?"

I got coffee. Kix flexed his fists, eager for milk.

"There was some of that."

"What a pleasant surprise it would be," said Stackhouse, "if one day soon the sheriff knew what was happening in her city."

"All important parties are alive and unharmed. An

uneasy truce was called between Ronnie and her detractors."

"And you?" he asked.

"No truce. Still working on that."

Timothy sighed. "I had hoped last night was the end."

"Soon," I said. "Darren won't leave town yet."

Stackhouse asked, "Darren What's-his-name, the prosecutor?"

"He and I have a score to settle. In the court room. And Grady Huff is the prize."

"That makes no sense."

"Doesn't to me either. And yet, here I am."

Manny arrived a few minutes later, wearing brown slacks and a checkered vest I didn't know he owned. His fingers and face glowed slightly pink, fresh from vigorous exfoliation.

He said, "Ay caramba, señorita, te ves atractivo en ese vestido. Tus senos se ven perfectos."

I translated, "He likes your nightgown, sheriff. And the woman underneath."

"Tell him thank you."

"We going to worship *Jesucristo*?" he asked.

"I am. Note my expertly affixed tie."

"Wait for me. I'll drive. First, un café negro."

Timothy and Stackhouse shared a glance. Manny going to church? For purposes of protection? Perhaps the danger to Timothy's son was greater than he expressed.

I said, "Everyone look how rugged and toothsome my son is. I mean, come on."

~

ST. JOHN'S EPISCOPAL WAS DOWNTOWN, a beautiful stone

church with original mahogany in the chapel, polished and gleaming. Stained glass windows, hanging cathedral lights, candles, the Christian flag, St. John's had it all. Manny and I slid into Marcus's pew a couple minutes late and took a hymnal.

He whispered, "Good of you to dress up. Least Manny, he put on a vest."

Between verses of *How Great Thou Art*, I said, "Perhaps you didn't note my tie."

"This charcoal suit cost me two grand, August. I got style."

"I don't peddle cocaine for a living," I said. "Fewer funds."

He whispered. "Maybe keep your voice down."

"About the cocaine? You bet."

His wife Courtney, singing in the choir, gave us a 'Hush!' motion, mid-chorus.

"Your wife is a knock out," I said.

"I know."

"Aren't you glad we're friends? We're so witty."

Manny shushed us. "Shut up, you two. I'm singing."

Marcus tilted his head to indicate the other side of the aisle. I followed his gaze.

Darren Robbins and Toby Moreno stood dutifully with hymnals in their hands, singing. Each wore an overcoat. Each had a slight pistol bulge at the hip. Toby saw me, raised his finger, and shot me with it.

The message was clear—this isn't over. We're still here.

"Those inauthentic pricks," I said softly. "Apostates. I should report their hypocrisy to a deacon."

"I got word this morning," said Marcus, "From an associate. Darren about ready to go home. He or Toby don't pop you soon, he'll put a price on your head."

"Heavens."

Another minute passed and Ronnie Summers slid next to Marcus from the other side of the pew.

I ogled her. So did everyone else.

Fat Susie absorbed the rest of the free space at the end.

"Thank you for the invite, Marcus," she said sweetly and softly, like a breeze in May. "Sorry I'm late. Reginald's hair takes forever."

She winked at me.

Thereafter I no longer had the ability to concentrate. I tried to focus on the words but they all turned to plucky Ronnie Summers.

We sat. After a while the sermon began.

Marcus wasn't happy about it, but I forced him to pass a note to Ronnie.

It said, ***Last night was impressive. We would've lassoed the moon, had you asked.***

She replied, ***Thank you. I cried for an hour afterwards. A year ago I would not have had the strength. If you were sitting beside me, I would hold your hand.***

I wrote back, ***That's episcopal fornication.***

She responded, ***Wouldn't it be hot if we fooled around during church?***

I began a reply but Manny took the slip of paper from my hands and ripped it in half.

Marcus mumbled, "About time. I was gonna do it soon. White people be passing notes in church, like when I was a boy."

"That's racist," I said.

28

Monday morning, Candice Hamilton and I dropped our kids off at the same time. Roxanne, dressing a little cuter than she used to, accepted them both.

We walked back to our cars and I said, "Why do girls dress better for each other than for outrageously attractive men?"

"Because we're judgmental bitches," said Candice. The chill had returned and she had a double-breasted overcoat synched with a belt. Her words produced vague steam.

"I knew it."

"Have any fun this weekend? I was hoping you'd call. Invite me out on the town."

"My weekend was mostly work," I said. "Nothing I would call fun."

"Let's get lunch."

"Alejandros," I suggested. "I need Mexican."

She smiled, forming the laugh lines. "It's a date."

I HAD a visitor waiting at my office. He sat on a chair in the hallway, staring at his phone. Bill Osborne, a twitchy prosecutor who worked for the Commonwealth's office.

"Inspector August," he said. "Got a minute? I have a confidential story to relate."

"Come into my office, Osborne. Been a while. Not since you helped me with Calvin Summers' informant."

He followed me in and I started the space heater.

"Correction. I didn't help at all. I couldn't or I'd be disbarred."

"That's what I meant," I said.

He sat. Looked at his phone, ran his finger across the screen a few times, and jerked his shoulders.

"I work in the Commonweath's office," he said. "I went in last night for a few hours. I don't get paid enough for that, but the government doesn't care. Anyway. Who did I run into? Phil Mason."

"Phil Mason," I said. "He's the prosecutor working on the Grady Huff case. He and Candice Hamilton locking horns."

"Exactly."

"Phil enjoying Darren Robbins lurking over his shoulder? I bet he loves that," I said.

"In fact he is not enjoying it. Co-counsel, not a smooth ride." He glanced at his phone a moment, as if temporarily distracted. "So anyway. Phil Mason is raging last night. He got a call from Judge Barker."

"Judge Barker, overseeing the Grady Huff trial, set to start in less than two weeks."

"Judge Barker is livid, apparently. And a little spooked. Judge Barker expressed indirectly to Phil that he's getting pressure about the Grady Huff trial," he said. "I heard you were involved and figured you for the aggravator."

"Judge Barker is feeling pressured," I repeated.

"To send Grady Huff away for life. Which, of course, makes him want to do the opposite."

"Who is in position to pressure a judge?"

"No one really," said Bill Osborne and he grinned. "The only person I can figure is the congressman. He's the guy who picks judges. But why would he care about Grady Huff?"

"Why indeed," I said.

Because Darren Robbins was exerting some power. His squad had contacted the congressman who had then contacted the judge.

He'd lost Ronnie.

He'd lost at poker, a game with totemic aftermath.

And now he fretted about losing the Grady Huff sentencing, which hitherto had been meaningless. But if he lost, he'd have struck out.

So he tried pressuring the judge. Little did he know Judge Barker was not a man to be pressured.

"So Mack," said Bill Osborne. "What the hell are you doing that's got Judge Barker and the Commonwealth's attorney so riled up?"

"I'm merely essaying my winning personality."

"That what you call it?"

"That and blindly pestering innocent citizens."

He said, "Well the locals are suddenly sick of this thing. This trial had a lot of energy and buzz, but I predict today it'll be nothing but gloom and doom. Phil's tired of the big shot attorney from Washington, and Judge Barker is gonna be prickly," he said.

"Does Phil want a plea?"

He twitched and glanced at his phone. "Hell yeah he wants a plea. I don't know the ins and outs, but he said the problem is the defendant won't plead and Darren Robbins wouldn't accept it anyway."

I said, "That's it exactly. Neither side wants a plea. Whereas yours truly wants to make it happen against their will. Coerce them into it."

"What role you playing? You're on the defense payroll?"

I nodded sagely. "Something like that."

"Shouldn't his attorney be coercing the plea deal? Why do you care?"

"I hate Darren Robbins. It's become personal. And something went down on the dock when Grady Huff killed his cleaning lady, and I want to find out what. Grady doesn't have the guts to pop someone without reason."

He nodded and checked his phone. "You're an interesting guy, Mack."

"My ways are inscrutable. Unable to be scruted."

"That's the word at the water cooler. How will you coerce them?"

I continued to nod, projecting investigatorial fluency. "Got no idea."

I PAID A FEW BILLS. Contacted a former client who still owed me money. Answered emails. Checked voice mail. Stewed. Had a sip of Johnny Walker Blue. Stewed some more. Thought about Veronica Summers. Pondered Candice Hamilton, but returned to Ronnie.

I wondered what she was doing at this moment. Probably sitting in her office, thinking about me. She'd be crazy not to.

Without anything better to do until lunch, I decided to pester Juanita Yates's mother. I'd tried to leave her out of this —her daughter had been murdered, after all. But she knew more than she let on. She knew her daughter was seducing and extorting men, and she hadn't told me. Heck, she'd tried to seduce me herself.

Could it be a family business? There was an interesting idea.

It was a cold day so I pulled on my driving gloves, as any proper gentleman worth a damn would. And I was worth several damns.

I'd parked on Campbell, halfway to 2nd Street. As I neared my car I saw something familiar. A black sedan, the plates removed. It had once tried to run me over.

Darren Robbins's goon squad?

There was an alley between the Total Action building and a vacant storefront. I passed it, blithely focusing on the sedan. From out of that alley, I was grabbed by strong hands and hauled in.

The day was cold. No one outside, no one on the sidewalk saw my disappearance.

Someone weighty and strong hit me in the stomach. It was a good one, a big hand, lots of force. A professional gut punch was no joke. A second someone hit me in the face. Not as good, but it hurt. Made my vision go blurry.

I fell over backwards and rolled away.

Got to my feet.

"Ooww," I said. More of a manly wheeze.

I retreated, hands raised defensively.

Two men stood there. Hispanic. Beefy. Heavy black hair. Frowns. Mean.

"You're not Darren Robbins's goons," I said and I spit into the alley. Only a little blood. "Wait, wait. Let me guess. Juanita Yates's two brothers. You've been following me."

"You done, white man," said the smaller of the two. He

shoved his finger at me with each syllable. "You go away. Finish."

I kept backing away, head ringing. Stomach spasming.

"Tu hablas español?"

"Sí. Y Mi hermana está muerta," he said.

My sister is dead.

"Lo sé," I said. "Lo siento."

I know. I'm sorry.

"Por qué faltas el respeto a los muertos?"

"Necesito saber qué pasó," I said. I stopped at a little cross section in the alley, where the adjacent buildings brought their trash. It was darkish but I had space.

They asked, *Why do you disrespect the dead?*

Because I need to know what happened.

"Dejala sola. O te mataremos," said the smaller of the two, still pointing.

Leave her alone or we'll kill you.

"Juanita?"

"Sí," he said.

"O Carlotta?" I asked.

"Ambos," he said. "Ella es mi hermana."

Both. She was my sister.

He said, "Te lastimaremos. Como lastimamos al gordo."

We'll hurt you like we hurt the fat guy.

"Grady?" I asked. "You messed up Grady Huff?"

"Sí, gordo y feo."

Yeah, fat and ugly.

Well well. How about that.

The things Grady hid from me were not insignificant.

I glanced around. This was a good place to make a stand. Besides, I had spontaneously and brilliantly developed a plan. And it was so good I scared myself.

"No puedes matarme. Mira mis enormes músculos," I said.

You can't kill me. Look at my huge muscles.

They laughed.

I laughed.

Look at us, best pals.

Or my Spanish wasn't working as well as I envisioned.

"Usted trabajó con su hermana. Para obtener dinero de sus novios. Pero no puedes asustarme, amigos," I said.

You and your sister worked together to take money from men, but you don't scare me.

"Eres un tipo grande. Pero te mataremos," he said.

You're a big guy but we can kill you.

"Prove it," I said.

"Dejala sola."

Leave her alone.

"No," I said.

The big guy had enough. When in doubt, punch people. So he did.

It was a slow and ludicrous punch. I didn't even try to block it. I stepped out of the way, as Fred Astaire might.

"No, no," I said. "Quick jabs. You strong guys learn bad habits."

I bobbed him on the nose. His eyes immediately watered and he stepped back.

His little brother threw a punch that landed in my ribs.

It hurt but not like he wanted.

I twisted, an uppercut with my elbow. Landed it into his teeth and he staggered away.

These guys weren't used to people hitting back.

A door opened—the rear exit to Leonore's. A cook froze there, his bag of trash forgotten.

"What's going on," he said.

"I'm being attacked," I replied. "It's terrifying."

"Should I…should I call the cops?"

"No," said the little brother.

"Quick as you can," I replied. "And please express my dismay."

The guy nodded but seemed undecided. I made a shooing motion and he ran inside.

"Vamonos," said the little brother, waving.

"Wait," I said. "You guys beat up Grady Huff, right?"

"Grady mató a mi hermana," said the big guy. First time he talked.

Grady killed my sister.

"I know," I said. "And now you're protecting yourselves and your mother. I get it. Era demasiado fuerte para ti?"

Grady too tough for you?

"Lloró como una niña pequeña," said the big guy.

He cried like a little girl.

"You hate Grady. You beat him up," I repeated. I wanted to hear it again. It was music, sweet music—the key to everything.

"Sí, y te mataremos, gringo."

And we'll kill you, white man.

"Listen, I have such a good idea," I said. "It'll be great. But you need to wait for the police."

The little guy made a motion. They turned for their car.

I grabbed the big guy by the jacket.

This time he surprised me. Got me good, a hard left I didn't see coming. I crashed into the brick wall.

Ouch. Whoops.

"Jose, tenemos que irnos," said the little brother impatiently, anxious to flee.

The big guy Jose turned to go. Doggedly I grabbed his jacket.

I was ready. He swung and missed.

"C'mon," I said, and I dabbed at the blood trickling from my right eyebrow. "You have to respect how tenacious and committed I am. Stick around. It'll be great. You'll go to jail and everything."

I snatched the little guy's jacket. He shoved me but I didn't let go. Jose tackled me from my blindside. Still I didn't release, dragging the little guy down with me. We all three collapsed.

Soon we were a writhing biracial heap on the alley bricks. One of those ugly scrums, desperate and discordant and furious, entirely without grace or talent. I kept the little brother in a headlock and dodged Jose as best I could. They were hurting me but couldn't injure me—big difference.

"Don't you want to hear my plan?" I croaked, ducking Jose again. "It's so good, though."

My modus operandi was to frustrate their efforts to retreat by any means necessary. Which I managed for several aggravating and angry minutes.

Long enough for the police to arrive. Shouts and sirens and blue lights.

The three of us were hauled apart. Pressed into the grimy alley walls, my arms pinned behind me.

"Took you long enough," I wheezed and coughed. "Someone call Sheriff Stackhouse. She'll get a kick out of this. Oh man, my plan is so good."

29

The next morning, as I entered the smelly jailhouse conference room, Grady Huff was waiting for me instead of vice versa. He was sitting at our usual metal table, heavily, wearing orange and cuffs. The room was empty except for two deputies standing expectantly in the corner.

"Where the hell have you been, fatty?" he asked. "I been waiting...for...why are you limping?"

"Sorry I'm late," I said. "Moving a little slow."

"Damn, Matt. Why do you have a brace on your knee? And what happened to your face?"

"First off, it's Mackenzie," I said, and I lowered gingerly onto the metal bench across from him.

"I don't care. The hell happened to you?"

"I got jumped in an alley. Twisted my knee and got my head busted up," I said.

I wasn't lying. A significant portion of my corporeal person ached. It looked worse than it felt. Because I am sturdy and rugged.

"By who?"

"We'll get to that, Grady Huff. First, let me tell you what you're going to do. And then second, I'll tell you why," I said.

"Where's Candice?"

"Shut up. You're going to strike a plea deal."

He frowned, which kinda pressed his whole face together. "No'm not."

"You confessed to the murder yet you insist you're innocent. It won't work. The jury is going to hate you. We need to plead," I said.

"Won't do it."

"You will plead for a crime of passion and/or self-defense, depending on what the Commonwealth attorney says."

"There wasn't any passion, *fatty*. I'm rich," he said.

"You'll still be in jail a long time, Grady Huff, you big dumb idiot. But less time. Now, secondly, here's why you're going to do it—I figured out what happened on that dock."

"No you didn't."

"Yes. I did," I said. I hoped.

"Nuh uh."

"Clever banter. You and Juanita became an item. Shut up. Listen. You were together. It was important to you. Lots of passion. It got hot. You two started skinny dipping at the dock."

Grady opened his mouth to protest but didn't.

I continued, "At some point, she sprang her trap on you. The same way she's done to her other lonely clients. Pay me, she demanded, or I'll expose you. Here's the part I don't understand, which you can clue me in on. Or not. I think you refused to pay. At first I assumed you would have happily paid Juanita but now the evidence suggests otherwise."

Grady remained stoic. His breathing rattled.

"But that part," I said, "is not important. What matters is this: her brothers showed up. They wanted money and they smacked you around. Two or three times? Enough so that you bought a gun. Your pride and frailties wouldn't let you call the police. You'd be exposed—you'd fallen in love with your cleaning lady. Egad, what would your *friends* think?"

Grady's chest began expanding and deflating to a greater degree.

"It's easy to buy a gun, Grady. But it's hard to use it to kill someone. So here's what I think happened next. Juanita returns, maybe under the guise of reconciliation. She's affectionate again. You two are reunited. She seduces you down to the dock. More skinny dipping? Who could say no to that. Except her brothers are waiting."

Now Grady's breathing accelerated and became shallow.

"My guess is, they were threatening to drown you. It's a way to scare and torture victims, the threat of drowning. I've seen it done. They can drop you in the water and let you scream, because you don't make a sound under the surface. Then pull you back up and do it again. That's it, right? They threatened to drown you. So you realize, the brothers mean business this time. Juanita had betrayed you, getting you to the water, and now you truly might die. Your life is in danger. You panic. This is serious enough to warrant pulling a trigger," I said. "You pull your gun. You fire. And aiming a pistol with shaking hands is difficult."

"The stupid spics were on my property," he said in a squeak, and a tear leaked from his right eye. His face was turning red and pitiful. "They had no right."

"You shot at them," I said. "And you missed."

He placed his hand over his mouth. Smothered a sob.

"The gunshot was loud," I continued. "I read the report. Three neighbors called 911. Juanita's two brothers had no choice but to run, before the police showed. By then Juanita was dead, killed accidentally."

"I didn't..." he whispered, shaking his head. "I didn't...it was..."

"It was self-defense gone wrong," I said. "You missed your target."

"No. No. Who would be..." He stopped, eyes closed, took a shuddering breath. "...who would be pathetic enough to fall in love with a...with a cleaning lady? Who would be pathetic enough to let two stupid poor *Mexicans* scare him? Who's dumb enough to shoot his girlfriend on accident? Not me, fatty."

The outside door opened and a lawyer hurried in. Same guy as before, cheap suit, kinda sweaty. He flattened his hair and laid his briefcase on the table. Adjusted his tie and cleared his throat. Shot us a weak smile while he waited for his new clients to arrive.

I said, "Why didn't you keep paying Juanita? She wanted money, right? I'm surprised you didn't fork it over. You're rich, after all."

"Guys like me," he sniffed. "Guys like my friends. We got women for days. We don't pay."

I said, "You've got a hurricane of emotions about this, Grady. I know. Guilt, anger, pride, hurt, remorse, fear. You can't let the pride win, though. You need to tell the truth. It'll save you years in jail," I said.

"Not me. I would never..."

"Juanita fooled other guys. Smarter guys. You shouldn't let—"

He slammed both hands on the metal table, the cuffs banging. "She didn't fool me! Get it through your *fat* head! She *loved* me. I know she did. Her stupid brothers ruined *every*thing!"

"It'll be hard to prove, but I think we can," I said. "Could we convince a jury? I don't know. But it's enough to strike a deal."

He shook his head. Sniffed. Snot running.

"She's dead," I said. "And it's at least partially her brothers's fault. They need to pay."

"I own part of Pepsi. *Pepsi!* Guys like me and my friends, we don't get lonely. No one gets to boss us around. We don't strike plea deals confessing to being afraid of Mexicans, *fatty*."

"So you're content to sit in prison? Even if you don't have to?" I said.

"The jury will see reason. I'm a celebrity. Guys like me, we're treated differently," he said and he wiped his eyes, smearing the tears under his glasses. "And if I stay in here a while? So what. I kinda like it. Guards are nice. Making some new friends."

"One of the problems with money," I said. "Is that it makes you stupid."

"How would you know? You're poor. Poor and fat."

"Nothing I can do to change your mind? A mature person is one who changes and grows. Their opinions and views evolve with the introduction of new evidence," I said.

"Not changing my mind. So quit asking. Quit asking and bring me a girl, why don't you. Make your fat self useful."

The inner door behind Grady opened. Two more deputies entered. They took their place in the corner, next to the original two. Four staunch deputies total, hands on their tactical utility belts, couldn't tell them apart to save my life.

The lawyer's two clients shuffled in. Orange and cuffed.

Grady turned to glance at the incoming prisoners.

He made eye contact with them. They froze.

Juanita's two brothers. They'd been here less than twenty-four hours.

The room reacted like a bomb went off. Grady screamed in terror. Scrambled to his feet and tripped over the table leg. The two brothers roared and attacked him. The four deputies, alerted against this possible reaction, began hauling the brothers back.

The sweaty guy in the suit looked like a man suddenly aspiring to become a tax attorney.

Grady screamed, "What the hell, get these guys off me!"

Which we did. Jose and his younger brother were dragged out of the room like rabid dogs, but not before knocking Grady into the wall. They shouted and raged at him, and he hid white-faced behind our table.

"Damn it," he said. He wiped his mouth and whimpered. "Damn it, Matt, what are they doing here?"

"Those two fellows?" I asked pleasantly. "They're the two goons who jumped me in the alley."

"You're shitting me."

"Nope."

"They jumped you? That's why you're torn up?"

"Yessir. Apparently they're still mad about their sister being shot. And they might be here a while."

Grady was kneeling on the floor. He took hold of my jacket with shaking hands.

"They can't stay," he said. "They *can't*."

"Wow, what if you and the two brothers draw the same shower schedule?" I wondered. "Golly."

"No. God, no. No that can't happen. They'll kill me, Matt."

"Mackenzie. You dope."

"Call the warden. We gotta fix this," said Grady Huff. His

face pressed into my jacket. He used it like a tissue. Not ideal. "I got money. We can...we can do something."

"It's a jail, Grady. It's not a nice place. Nor is it a safe place. Stuff like this happens," I said. "Jeez, the things I've seen..."

"I'll pay you. Anything you want."

"You already are paying me."

"But we...we gotta....oh my God."

"I got an idea. Strike a deal. Today," I said.

He didn't respond.

"You plead to crime of passion or self-defense. You get less time behind bars. The two brothers might get what they deserve. And part of the deal? You get shipped immediately to a better prison."

"Fine."

"Yeah?" I said.

"Fine, whatever, fatty, just get me out of here."

"Hah," I said. Victoriously. "Wait till Darren hears this."

"Who? What?"

"I said, You're welcome. For protecting you from yourself."

30

An hour later, Sheriff Stackhouse and Candice Hamilton met me in the front hallway of the Roanoke County's Circuit Courthouse on East Main. Stackhouse drew a crowd wherever she went and today was no different. She was holding forth to an adoring audience of lawyers and cops. I caught her eye and she excused herself.

Candice asked me, "Grady will plead? I promised Phil Mason I'd have something."

"The brothers scared him silly. We're in business."

Stackhouse punched me in the arm. "A dirty trick, babe. I'm proud. You'd make a good sheriff."

We went around the corner and down a side hall. Stackhouse smiled at the guards and Candice flashed her bar card and we bypassed security. Judge Barker's receptionist waved us through.

Stackhouse knocked on the wooden door and we pushed inside.

Barker's chambers did not befit his near omnipotence. Old books, disorganized white binders, two faded framed photographs, cheap furniture.

"Come in, Stackhouse. Come in, Ms. Hamilton," he called, standing from behind his desk. The man himself struck an imposing figure—six feet-two inches, maybe, two hundred pounds, looked like he still swam a couple miles every day despite being sixty. Bald as could be.

Stackhouse went to the desk and kissed Barker on the cheek. "Morning, doll."

Barker didn't mind. He said, "What's so damned important we need an emergency conference, counselor?"

Phil Mason—young, ersatz beard, glasses, blonde hair, bad posture—stood with Darren Robbins on the other side of the judge's chamber. Next to imposing and handsome Robbins, Phil looked like a newborn. Batman and Robin. Except stupid.

"Good morning, your honor," said Candice Hamilton. "We need an immediate injunction on behalf of the defendant, and I think we might strike a deal."

"Injunction." Darren Robbins said the word like it was cute. "On what grounds?"

"He was attacked in prison. By the siblings of Juanita Yates," said Candice.

"Bull shit. What siblings?"

"Language," grunted Judge Barker.

Darren said, "Allegedly attacked. Any witnesses?"

"Seven. Plus cameras."

Judge Barker turned baleful eyes on me. "You helped Brad Thompson. August, right? The hell happened to you?"

"The same two brothers who attacked Grady Huff, they also attacked me. That's why they were in prison in the first place," I said.

"And why we need Mr. Huff moved."

Darren scoffed. "How convenient. They allegedly attacked you."

Stackhouse winked at him. "I'll vouch. I got to the scene quickly."

"And then you turned the angry prisoners loose on the defendant," said Darren. "Mistreatment of a prisoner. I need to speak with Mr. Huff immediately."

"I'll see what I have on my calendar, Darren," Candice said sweetly. "Maybe sometime next week? In the mean time, I need him moved."

Phil Mason spoke for the first time. "He wants to plead?" His voice squeaked only a little.

"There'll be no plea deal," Robbins answered. "Grady confessed."

"Circumstances change," said Candice.

Judge Barker's arms were crossed and he looked between us unhappily. "New evidence?"

"Your honor, I've had no time for discovery. The trial is only—"

"I'd like to hear from the defense, please, Mr. Robbins."

Barker nodded at Candice.

She said, "If it suits you, I'll let Mr. August talk. He's the investigator I hired to follow up on the sordid details."

Darren rolled his eyes at the word sordid.

"Go ahead, Mr. August," said Barker.

"Want the facts straight?" I asked. "Or in short story form?"

Judge Barker thought about smiling. But he didn't.

"Why not. Short story," he said.

"The victim, Juanita Yates, was a professional con artist," I began, assuming a winsome tone.

"Bull shit," said Darren again. "Your honor, this—"

"Be quiet, Mr. Robbins, or you'll be outside."

Darren's head nearly exploded.

I started over. "Juanita Yates was a professional con

artist. She cleaned the houses of forlorn bachelors, and the occasional lonely married man, and gradually seduced her feckless targets. I have three men ready to testify, four if you include Grady Huff."

It was only a partial bluff. Mostly true. Or at least, not entirely false. None of the men had agreed to testify under oath but they existed.

"Feckless," said Barker. "Go on."

"Juanita Yates might not be her real name because most of the men know her as Carlotta. She worked her charms and in all cases the professional relationship turned amorous. Each man ready to testify was intimate with her. Juanita convinced them to skinny dip with her, which her brothers videotaped. This videotape was used to blackmail her clients. If her client balked, the brothers threatened harm. In Grady's case, harm was in evidence."

"This is absurd," said Darren. "Why would the defendant not reveal this earlier?"

Candice said, "You'd need to spend time with him, your honor. Mr. Huff's a special case. Almost unfit to stand trial. Simply put, he's incompetent, embarrassed, ignorant, and foolish."

"You said short story," Barker reminded me.

"Long story short, Juanita was sexually aggressive as a profession, and in cahoots with her siblings. She and Grady became intimate. He fell in love. She attempted extortion, which triggered his deep insecurities and racism. The brothers smacked him around and threatened to kill him. Grady bought a gun. They returned. He fired, he missed, he shot Juanita by mistake."

Darren Robbins groaned. "An accident? No way. Again, why wouldn't the defendant reveal this?"

"He has crippling self-doubt," I said. "He cannot admit

his weaknesses, not even his bad aim. But it happened and it makes him feel kinda important."

"This is a damned mess," growled Barker.

"You think a jury would buy that cockamamie story?"

Candice said, "It'll be child's play proving Grady was tricked by a professional con artist. As for the bad aim? We might not even need to."

Phil Mason the feeble prosecutor said, "You have the names and numbers of her former clients?"

"I do," I said.

"Her brothers are in custody, having attacked both you and Mr. Huff?" asked Mason.

Stackhouse nodded. "They are."

"Mr. Huff wants to plead?"

"He does," said Candice.

Mason and Judge Barker glanced at one another. The implications were apparent—they both wanted this gone.

"But he *confessed*," growled Robbins.

"He'll confess under oath to self-defense," said Candice. "He'll confess his heart was broken, that he wasn't in his right mind, that the love of his life betrayed him, that he feared for his safety, that he was being attacked, and that his aim was bad."

"I will destroy that fat bastard on the stand," said Darren.

"That's a damned unprofessional thing to say, sir," said Barker.

"Your honor, I think the community and its leaders would like to see justice done. This trial is about the rich and privileged being held accountable for the mistreatment of the working class. This verdict matters. That's why I'm donating my time. The congressman himself—"

"I don't give a hill of beans about that pompous tulip.

Tell him I said so. Mr. Mason, your thoughts?" asked Judge Barker.

"Your honor—"

"Close your mouth, Mr. Robbins, or I'll sanction you all the way back to Washington."

"In his defense, your honor," I said. "Mr. Robbins is a nitwit."

Phil Mason cleared his throat. "I need to take depositions, your honor. At least from Mr. August and Mr. Huff. If the testimonies corroborate, we'll meet her prior clients and the two brothers. I anticipate the Commonwealth will recommend a plea deal. Manslaughter, maybe."

"Manslaughter?" Robbins nearly shouted. "He bought a gun, shot the poor woman, and then confessed!"

Barker roared, "Quiet, Mr. Robbins!"

"A miscarriage of justice from a bunch of fucking rookies," snapped Darren Robbins. He stormed across the room and fled, the door slamming behind.

A moment of silence.

Stackhouse grinned. "Want me to bring him back, your honor?"

"No. I like it better with him gone."

Candice nodded at Phil Mason. "Let's go talk, Phil. Your honor, thank you for your time. Meanwhile, about Mr. Huff's safety?"

Barker sighed and grumbled. "Sheriff?"

Stackhouse winked at him. "No problem. I'll get the brothers transferred today."

"Good. Good," said Barker. "Come back with your decision, counselors. That invitation does not extend to Mr. Robbins."

~

THE FOUR OF us paused on the courthouse steps between the wide columns. A northern wind was swirling down East Main, tearing leaves off the oak tree.

Darren Robbins waited there. He put his hand on my shoulder.

"You're a real pain, August."

"I know this," I said.

Sheriff Stackhouse gave Darren Robbins a swat on the ass and she went down the steps. "So long, Washington big shot. Don't let the door hit you on the way out."

Darren watched her go, still gripping my shoulder.

"That woman cannot possibly be the sheriff," he said.

"Time for you to go home, Darren. You struck out here."

"I did," he said. With a surprising amount of grace. "You got me on all counts."

I frowned at him. Suspiciously and handsomely.

Candice said, "Phil, let's schedule emergency depositions for tomorrow. Trial is not far and I want this settled."

Phil, still hangdog despite being on the verge of offloading the toxic Grady Huff case, shrugged. "Yeah, I can do that. We'll confirm some details, but this shouldn't be an issue."

I made to move but Darren held tight.

"Leggo."

"What's your hurry," he said. "Got another issue I want to discuss."

"Don't care."

"Well," he said and paused. He was searching for ideas.

Holding me in place.

Keeping me still.

My inner alarms rang.

"Maybe we wait until Candice and Phil move on," he said. "And talk."

This was a setup.

A gun fired. I saw the flash in my periphery, roof across the street, second floor of the Marine recruiting station.

The shot missed. Maybe it hit the branches of the oak tree. Maybe the wind blew it off course.

Candice screamed. So did Phil.

I lunged into Darren, knocking us both down the wide concrete steps.

"You sonofabitch," he snarled in my ear. "Why can't you die."

I'd gotten close.

More gun shots. Two of them. Misses. The steps nearby cracked.

Aiming a gun accurately is harder than people assume.

I was up and darting across the courthouse lawn.

Movement on the roof. Shooter retreating, I bet.

I pulled my Kimber 1911 from the shoulder holster.

Sheriff Stackhouse was charging back, gun drawn. She moved well.

"Shooter on the roof," I shouted.

I went into East Main. A car swerved but hit me anyway, a glancing blow. I tumbled to the street. Got up. Hurled an imprecation. Retrieved the dislodged Kimber and finished crossing East Main with a pronounced limp.

Embarrassing. James Bond never gets hit by cars.

I came around the corner of the recruiting station into the parking lot next to Mac & Bobs restaurant.

Early lunch patrons were scattering, crying.

Toby Moreno and I arrived simultaneously. Front and back of the parking lot. He held an assault rifle. Getaway car had to be close.

"August!"

He raised the rifle.

I fired from the hip and his windbreaker jacket jerked and puckered. He staggered backwards. Stayed up, trying to aim.

From his blindside, another shooter opened fire. Three blasts from short range, no misses, caught Toby in the torso and hurled him to the blacktop. The sound caromed back and forth on the brick walls.

More screaming, pedestrians on the sidewalk.

Carlos stepped out of his old grey pickup, gun smoking.

"Señor August, you are okay," he called.

"Yeah," I said. "Hit by a car. Don't tell anyone."

I knelt beside Toby. He was already half gone, not long for this world. His eyes searching but not seeing. On the blacktop beside him, an AR-15.

"Carlos, what are you doing here," I said, panting a little.

"The bastards. I knew they would try. Marcus, he say I could follow you."

"A great idea," I said and stretched my knee. "I owe you big."

"No, Señor August. I am still in your debt."

The sheriff arrived. She saw Toby and shouted orders, "Stay inside! Everyone inside!" Then she got on her radio.

Carlos said, "I was too late. I am sorry, señor August."

"Right on time, Carlos. Saved the day."

"No, migo. I saw it from my truck."

"Saw what?"

"He missed you," said Carlos. He pointed past me. "But the girl, the lawyer. The bullet got her."

31

Candice Hamilton had been shot in the chest. The rifle bullet meant for me had pulverized her ribs and liquified the lower half of her right lung. She was lucky—only two miles from Lewis Gale Hospital. Stackhouse carted her there in a squad car in under three minutes despite the traffic. I sat in the back, holding Candice on her side, pressure on the wound to keep the lung inflated.

Stackhouse and I held vigil in the waiting room, holding hands. Took an hour before we stopped shaking.

She asked quietly, "Darren set it up?"

"Yeah. I was the target."

She released some air slowly and leaned her head back against the wall.

Finally a surgeon came out to tell us, "The problem is the bullet's tumbling effect. It ricocheted inside, causing extra damage. We'll know more tomorrow."

I left the hospital at dinner, unsure if she'd live.

I visited the following day but she was still sedated. I deposited flowers on her window sill.

Stackhouse called me Wednesday with an update.

"Hamilton will survive," she told me. "Though she'll never run marathons again."

"Did she ever?"

"I don't care, kiddo. She's in an ambulance, headed to Johns Hopkins. Told me to tell you goodbye."

"Ironic, no?" I said. "Both she and Juanita Yates, shot by accident. But Candice will live because she was shot near a hospital. Luck of the draw."

"Candice was surrounded by good people. Juanita was shot trying to blackmail a fat and insecure lonely man. Sometimes these things make a difference, babe," she said.

"You're suggesting we're the result of the accumulation of our choices?"

"You know, a handsome guy like you shouldn't try so hard to be smart. What's for dinner?" she asked.

"It's Manny's turn."

"Thought so. I might take your father out."

I hung up. Crossed my sneakers on top of my desk (worn in case I had to limp after dastardly malfeasants) and reached into the bottom drawer for Johnny Blue.

It was a commendable day for an entire gulp.

I did just that and I said a prayer for Candice. Popped the cork back in and closed the drawer.

My laptop was open. A new request for my services open on screen.

I glared at it. Tried to read it. Tried again. Gave up.

I didn't want to think about it.

Not yet...

I WOKE up in that position, hypnagogia having snuck up like a thief in the night.

I wasn't alone.

Ronnie Summers bent at the waist, lowering over my chair. Slid her arms around my neck and pressed her lips against mine. We stayed that way, intimate and proprietary, a long while.

There are worse ways to waken.

Finally she released.

"Hello Mackenzie," she said, our noses still touching.

"Hello Ronnie."

"You smell like scotch."

"You smell like peppermint. And youthful vigor."

"I'm on my way to court," she said. "But I saw your car and grew prurient. Isn't that one of your words?"

"Yes," I said. "And now that you're here, I am concupiscent."

"Show off."

"More like raw talent."

"How's your knee?" she asked.

"Better. Only hurts when I run."

"I can't stay," she said. "I'm late. But I wanted to see you."

"Let's go on a date."

"Yes. A thousand times yes. This time, you and Reginald won't carry me home."

"He still with you?" I asked.

"No. Marcus informed me Darren returned to Washington. The threat of exposure called off my aggressors. Reginald has been released to Marcus—I'm safe. And apparently the undisputed queen of marijuana this side of Richmond," she said.

"Congratulations."

"I'm a big deal. Care for some free pot?"

"I do not," I said.

"I don't either. Which is a shame. I've got loads of the

stuff." She went to her bag. "I heard through the grapevine, Grady Huff pled to manslaughter."

"Probably as it should be. He's an ass but he didn't murder anyone in cold blood. What he really needs is an extremely tolerant and long-suffering and deaf girlfriend," I said. "And maybe she should be blind."

"Are you glad it's over?"

"I am. Made me a small fortune, though."

"Darren will never be connected to the Toby Moreno shooting."

"Even if we find witnesses who saw them together," I said. "He'll claim it was circumstantial. Nothing will stick. Darren is free and clear."

"He's not through with you."

"I know this. And I'm not through with him."

"Mackenzie," she said. Slow and reluctant. "I need to confess something. I lied."

"Always tell the truth. Or at least never lie," I said.

"You're quoting something. But anyway. That night at poker, when I set the files on the table, I said I didn't have a file for you. But, in reality, I do."

She pulled out an envelope, secured with folding tabs. Handed it to me. I stood.

"Before you open it," she said. "Please understand. I was scared about that night. I thought I would be killed. I thought you would be killed. And...it just happened."

I pressed the tabs together. Opened the envelope.

"Wait." She placed her hand on mine. Hers shook. "It doesn't mean anything. Please don't panic. I can fix it."

"Relax. We're okay," I said.

"Alright, but...okay. Look."

I pulled out a paper.

It was a marriage certificate. An official one.

A legal contract between Mackenzie August and Veronica Summers. We had both signed.

"Uh..." I said intelligently.

"I thought Darren was going to have me shot and I wanted you to receive all my possessions," she said in a rush. "Or I thought you would be shot and...well, damn it, I didn't want to completely lose Kix. I would have shared him with your father. I'd only take him on weekends."

"You and I...we're married?"

"It just...happened. I had it drawn up. Reginald knows people with weird talents," she said.

"It's real?"

"As far as the Commonwealth of Virginia is concerned. Since Friday."

"We're married," I repeated. Although it sounded like someone else said it. Someone from a movie. "That's a decent replication of my signature."

"I'll get it annulled. I swear I will. Don't be mad. But for the record, you're the only bachelor in Virginia who'd be upset married to me." She glanced at her watch. "I'm so late!"

"You're my wife," I said.

"Good grief, that sounds hot from those lips." She grabbed my shirt. Kissed me. Picked up her purse again. "I have to run."

"This went through the system?"

"Yes! Friday."

"I'm your husband," I said.

"Yes Mackenzie. Stop the dirty talk right now or I'll be held in contempt of court. Wow, I'm a mess. I *have* to go." She hurried to the door. "We'll talk tonight. Okay, my husband? After matrimonial consummation. Extreme honeymoon bliss. Maybe twice?"

She glanced at her watch again, yelped, and fled down the stairs.

The wedding certificate was still in my hands.

Glowing. Getting hotter.

"Sweet Jiminy Christmas."

THE END

~

WANT MORE MACKENZIE? Links are below.

Two Pages of...
My Opinion on...
The State of the Novel

John Grisham is still rich. He makes five million dollars per book, or whatever the huge number is. But he's making less now than he used to make per book. It used to be ten million. That's a good thing, in my opinion, for all of us, including him.

What changed?

Here's what the math looked like ten years ago for every hundred people who wanted to be writers:

1 person becomes John Grisham, ten million per book.
9 people traditionally publish books, making $5,000 per.
60 people try and fail to get their book published.
30 people never try, feeling defeated before they begin.

But then technology leveled the playing field.

Somewhat.

Thanks to the Kindle and eReaders, here's what the math looks like in 2018 for every hundred people who want to be a writer:

1 person becomes John Grisham, five million per book.
9 people traditionally publish, making $5,000 per book.
30 people self-publish books, making $10,000 per book.
30 people self-publish books, making $1,000 per book.
20 people try/fail to get their book traditionally published.
10 people never try, feeling defeated before they begin.

(Those numbers are approximate and should be taken as an indication of the truth, rather than cold fact)

I love the new numbers. More books get published, more people realistically chase their dream, and more people make a living writing or simply have a part-time job they adore.

Why is this good for John Grisham, who is making less? Fewer people are reading his books, after all. Because it increases the overall health of the writer/reader market. More people than ever are reading books, even on their phones. Newer writers mean more creative stories and better characters. John Grisham and the rest of us benefit as we push back against mindless games on our screens and the onslaught of Netflix sucking up our time.

It's a chaotic time in publishing.

Many things are changing.

But most of them are great for writers and readers.

This is a long way of saying...

...thank you, Kindle, for helping me have a career.

...thank you, reader, for taking a break from the literary giants and taking a chance on me.

I'm having a ball writing Mackenzie and Ronnie.

Want more?

1) August Origins (Book One)
2) Desecration of All Saints (Book One and a Half)
3) The Second Secret (Book Two)

4) Flawed Players (Book Three)
5) Last Teacher (Prequel - I'll email you the book for free)
6) Aces Full (Book Four. You just finished this book.)
7) Only the Details (Book Five)
8) Ghost in Paradise (Short Story. I'll email you.)
9) Good Girl (Book Six)
10) The Supremacy License (Manny/Sinatra, Book One)
11) Wild Card (Manny/Sinatra, Book Two)

Desecration and *Last Teacher* don't necessarily have to be read in order. Nor do the Manny/Sinatra books.
Are you having the time of your life reading these books?
Yes. Yes you are.
Is it only getting better?
Yes. Yes it is.
If I haven't email you the Prequel yet, now's a good time.

Author Acknowledgements

Guys like me only have a career thanks to you and your reviews on Amazon/GoodReads. Leave one, if you can.

Many thanks to Brad Thompson and Adam Moseley, founts of information. And to Kim Sarrell and Teresa Blecksmith and Clair, for being willing readers.

Check out Mackenzie on Audible - I think Scott Ellis does a great job. **https://www.audible.com/pd/Mysteries-Thrillers/Sophomore-Slump-Audiobook/B07BK84CZK**

SNEAK PEEK OF BOOK FIVE

Chapter One

"Jiminy Christmas," I said. Again.

I'd said it a lot that day but the phrase felt right. Don't tinker with a good thing.

I sat in my reclining swivel chair, feet planted firmly on the floor. I wanted to cross them on the desk like any respectable and debonaire detective would do, but my sneakers had been unresponsive for several hours, the cowards.

My laptop was open and impatient, beckoning for attention.

In my hands I held an official marriage certificate pinched gingerly on the edges between my fingertips, like it was hot.

It was *my* marriage certificate.

Whose marriage certificate?

Mine.

That's impossible, you say.

You're right it is. I'd never married anyone.

And yet...legally I had a wife.

I had a *wife*.

She was a humdinger, too. A dame worth killing for. An attorney who made a mean cocktail. She read books to children at the Rescue Mission and drove too fast through school zones. She adored my son and hinted about seducing my roommate. She'd never told me she loved me but she'd admitted it to a poker table full of professional malfeasants. Hard to decide if she looked more like royalty wearing an evening gown or black activewear.

A girl I deemed deserving of my dedication and devotion.

Did I want to marry her? I assumed so, yes. One day.

Though probably not yet.

However...here I sat. Contemplating the evidence of our union.

"Jiminy Christmas," I said.

My net worth had probably skyrocketed. So that was nice. And she'd mentioned marital consummation and honeymoon bliss as she dropped off the document earlier that day.

Did I desire honeymoon bliss?

Yes. Yes I did.

But did I deserve it?

Yes. Yes I did.

Someone knocked on my door.

If I was the kind of incompetent man who got startled, I would have been.

A cute girl stood there. Not a girl, but younger than me. Maybe twenty-five. She had one of those haircuts that looked feminine but didn't reach her ears. Blonde.

Untucked slim-fit checkered flannel shirt, sleeves rolled up. Jeans. Bright white teeth.

"Sorry to interrupt," she said.

"No you're not."

"You're right. I should say, I hope you don't mind if I disrupt your daydreaming."

"Better," I said. "More honest."

"You look like a man in a good mood. You were grinning at the ceiling."

"I do not grin. And if I did, it would be a volitional expression of good humor. Not the reflex of a milksop," I said.

"Jeez, okay. Why are you purposefully displaying your good humor?"

"I got married today."

"Oh wow. Congratulations!"

"Not necessary. It's easy to do, turns out. How can I help?"

"You're Mackenzie?"

"I am."

She pointed down the stairs. "I bought Metro. Or, the space next-door where Metro used to be. I was going to ask if you had five minutes to lend a hand, but seeing as it's your wedding day..."

I stood. Laid the marriage certificate carefully on my desk. Like it might eat me.

"I miss Metro. Their lunch menu was solid."

"Mine will be better," she said. "Guaranteed."

"What do you need help with?"

"The water main. I'd like to switch it on. So stupid but I can't find it. I'll give you a free lunch when we open next spring."

"Deal."

"Great. Thanks."

I came around the desk. She backed up, letting me descend the stairs first.

I grabbed the handrail.

"What's the name of your restaurant?" I asked.

She didn't answer.

And I realized my mistake...

Made in the USA
Las Vegas, NV
06 November 2023